Meeting at Carondelet

Enjoy my first book.
Frank Pamblanco

Frank Pamblanco

Copyright © 2020 Frank Pamblanco
All rights reserved.

ISBN 13: 9781520226866

DEDICATION

I dedicate this book to the women in my life. My mom Cuqui, my beautiful wife Terri, and my two gorgeous daughters Vanessa and Amanda. And to my nephew, the special person who inspired me to write this book.

1

The Winston family arrived at 4727 Merlot Circle. Their home sat in a cul de sac with only six other homes surrounding it. Painted a yellowish, almost mustard color, it was situated on an upscale middle-class gated community by the name of Eastwood Village. It was the home Lydia always wanted with the long semicircular driveway, tall perfectly trimmed row of bushes on both sides of the home, while at the same time the smell of fresh oleander roses announced the start of spring. As soon as Tom stopped the car Charlie jumped out from the back seat and ran towards the front door. He stood there staring at the door without saying a word until Tom let him in.

Charlie's room walls were full of posters. Posters from classic cars, posters from Michael Jackson. Posters from famous wrestlers and popular UFC fighters; although Lydia did not let him watch any of the bouts because she considered them too bloody and violent. As soon as Lydia stepped into the front door, she heard Charlie's loud and deep voice.

"I am hungry mom" he screamed all the way from his room. Then he yelled it twice again.

"Ok honey I heard you the first time. No need to scream, ok? We are ordering pizza in a few minutes."

"Ok mom." Charlie yelled from his upstairs room.

Lydia shook her head from side to side looking up towards Charlie's room, waiting for him to come running downstairs, give her a big hug, and say *'I love you mom'*. She waited for almost five minutes, but it did not happen. All she heard from his room was the loud voice of Michael Jackson singing *Beat it*.

Tom was at the kitchen putting away some of the groceries when Lydia walked in. She was still shaking her head and Tom noticed right away her red and teary eyes.

"Are you ok honey?" he asked her.

"I wish..." she started saying. "I wish he would..."

"What is bothering you Lydia?" Tom asked her as he put both his hands on her shoulders.

She started to sob some more and Tom tried to offer some consolation by rubbing her shoulders.

"I wish that he would tell me more often that he loves me, you know? Why can't he be more open and closer to me Tom?"

"I don't know honey. As the doctors said, autism is still a mystery in the medical world. They still do not know much about it."

"Why us Tom? Why us? Did I do anything wrong during my pregnancy?" she asked Tom crying.

"Please honey, don't torture yourself. It is not your fault that Charlie is the way he is. It was God's will." Tom answered her

"God's will?" she replied wiping some of her tears. "To hell with God then!" she added angrily.

She turned away from Tom and quickly ran upstairs to their bedroom.

"Lydia, Lydia! Come on, you don't mean that..." Tom said as he started following her upstairs.

But he let her go. There was no point. He knew that she needed to be alone at this time and that his company was not appreciated at this moment. As in many times before, she needed to calm her angry soul. He banged his fist on the kitchen counter a couple of times. "Shit...shit..." he said to himself.

Tom put away the rest of the groceries and afterwards headed towards the old grand piano that was located on the south corner of the formal living room. This was his favorite private place of their colonial style home they had purchased about five years ago. He glanced at the pictures on top of the Steinway & Sons grand piano. Pictures of their wedding, of Charlie, Lydia's parents, Lydia's sister Lily, Lydia's cousins, and his parents. He turned his attention to a very special picture he cherished most, one of him and his dad. It had been taken on a trip when they had traveled to Spain, almost exactly two years before he had died of stomach cancer. The grand piano had been a gift from his dad, the same piano where he had taken many lessons as a kid. Tom's mom was always asserting he was a genius, and that someday he was going to become a famous piano player, a composer, or both. She even convinced him to name his first child after the famous blind musician Ray Charles. It was not meant to be, but shortly after him and Lydia got married his dad and a moving truck appeared all of a sudden in front of their new home, piano in tow, as a special wedding gift for them.

"I know how much this piano means to you so I want you to have it, and pass it on to your kids" his dad had told him.

Tom caressed the frame of that special picture. The picture where Lydia always told him he looked like a young version of his dad.

"You look just like Mr. Raymond Winston on that picture Tom" she told him many times before.

Thomas E. Winston carefully picked up the picture from the old Steinway piano his dad had gifted to them on their wedding many years ago.

"It hasn't been easy dad; it hasn't been easy" he whispered to that special picture.

The First Sign
The sweet smell of the lavender roses infused into the kitchen as soon as Lydia opened the side hallway door that led to a small garden. She always wondered how these beautiful lilac roses smelled so sweet, and floral. The aroma of fresh brewed coffee and a clear morning sky

made it a perfect way to start the day, especially after the previous evening. She heard slow steps coming down the stairs.

"Hello precious!" said Tom peeking his head into the kitchen. "Feeling better today?" he asked.

Lydia was washing last night's dishes, her back towards Tom.

"Yes, I guess I am…"

"Honey," Tom started saying "you cannot keep beating yourself like that. It is not…"

"My fault?" Lydia unexpectedly interrupted him. She quickly turned around to face Tom.

Tom got closer to her and started caressing her soft right cheek.

"I am sorry about yesterday. I did not mean what I said" said Lydia

"I know" Tom replied to her.

"I am going to apologize to Charlie later".

"Honey, he didn't hear what you said."

"But I should apologize nevertheless. I should have not said those words to you or Charlie."

"Lydia" Tom started saying while lifting her chin. "We have to realize that our son is different and that he is not going to change"

"I know. I realize that. But it hurts inside sometimes" she said resting her right hand on her chest.

"You are a good mother Mrs. Winston" said Tom staring at her green eyes.

"You are a great father Mr. Winston" she replied to him.

"Now, go cook me some breakfast" said Tom slapping her rear.

"Hey, don't touch what is not yours!"

"Oh yes, it is. This is all mine!" replied Tom, this time grabbing her rear even tighter.

"You horny toad. Get out of here. I'll call you when breakfast is ready." She said as she pulled his arms away.

"Love you" Tom said to her.

"Love you too, you horny toad" she replied.

After Charlie's diagnosis with autism Lydia had decided not to have any more children. Tom on the other hand wanted at least three, having been raised in a large family. They had argued about this many times. They discussed the possibility of adoption but Lydia was not warm to that idea. Years passed, and as Charlie condition changed Tom understood and respected Lydia's decision.

They met each other during Tom's junior year in college while taking the same class. Lydia swept him of his feet from the first time she saw her at his class. She was petite, with beautiful long, auburn hair. He could not wait to attend that class every Thursday just to see Lydia. After about the fourth meeting of that semester Tom was ready to ask her out. But every time he tried, he had cold feet. What if she had a boyfriend already? What if she was married, with kids? He did not want to be left with a broken heart. Two weeks before the end of the semester Tom was at the library diligently studying for his finals. His head was down concentrated on his book when he heard a soft, female voice behind him.

"Hey, you" the voice said

Tom turned around. To his surprise, it was Lydia, standing right next to him.

Tom sat there perplexed staring at this gorgeous woman he had been admiring all the semester.

"When are you going to ask me out?" Lydia said

Tom did not say a word. He sat there as if the chair had been super glued to his buttocks.

"Here, this is my cell number"

Lydia handed him the note and Tom finally got a few words out.

"Yes, thank you! My name is..." Tom started to say.

"I know your name. We are in the physics class together. Well, have to go. See you later".

Still glued to his chair Tom admired her beautiful body as she exited the room. As it turned out, he wasn't the only one paying attention.

Two years later they were married. A year later Charles joined the family. She always planned to attend medical school but after Charlie's diagnosis they both agreed that one of them needed to stay home to care for Charlie's needs, at least until he was more mature. They decided that Lydia would be a full-time mom while Tom attended the FBI Academy in Quantico after he completed his criminal justice degree. Lydia was happy being a full-time mom, unlike many other women out there.

After finishing cooking dinner that evening Lydia was still feeling uneasy and somewhat guilty about her outburst at Tom. Although Charlie had not heard her comments or understood the situation, she felt compelled to talk to him alone and try to explain the reason she felt the way she did. Especially he wanted him to maybe, just maybe, understand that her frustration was not his fault. She quietly made her way upstairs towards Charlie's room. She immediately heard the voice of Joe Rogan, the UFC commentator blasting from his television. She opened the door quietly. The channel was showing UFC 138 and Rogan was interviewing one of the fighters prior to the main event. Lydia could not stand the violence, the open wounds, and the blood all over the octagon floor. In her opinion, this type of sport should be banned not only in Virginia, but the country as well. But Charlie loved the sport, watching at least three of the UFC shows per week.

But this evening Charlie was instead sitting in front of his small desk, his laptop computer open. Behind the desk was a small sliding window that peered into the neighbor's house. Charlie was not concentrated on the UFC bout, but rather was attentively looking thru the window. He was sitting towards the right side of his desk to get a better view outside. He had that usual smirk on his face.

"Charles, I told you I don't want you to watch these bloody fights. Ok?" Said Lydia

Charlie did not respond. Not even a twitch. He was strictly concentrated on whatever was outside his window.

"Charlie, did you hear me?" she asked again this time turning off the television.

"Charles, Charlie…what are you looking at?"

No response from him, he continued to peer outside that window as if in a trance.

Lydia got closer. She stood right behind him to get a better look and quickly realized what was grabbing Charlie's attention. By the neighbor's pool was Mayra, the sixteen-year-old neighbor's daughter calmly taking a sun tan after swimming at their pool minutes before. Charlie was staring directly at her, and she knew it. Mayra was staring back at Charlie, opening and closing her legs, licking her lips, while giving Charlie an innocent girly stare.

"Oh my God!" exclaimed Lydia covering his eyes with her hands "Charlie, please don't stare at that..." she started saying.

But Lydia could not complete her sentence. All of a sudden, her body turned cold, and her eyes felt so heavy she was forced to close them. She started talking as if in a trance herself.

"You little weirdo, yes, you can look all you want." Lydia started saying.

The words were coming out of her mouth but they felt as if they were not hers.

*"Do you like what you see? You like this, don't you? I bet you would love to fuck me...*Lydia said again*"You little weirdo. I'll fuck your dad instead!"* Lydia finished saying.

After that last sentence Lydia took two steps back away from Charlie. Her cold feeling went away. She felt as if she was about to lose consciousness, and barely landed on the edge of Charlie's bed. Lydia just sat there, speechless, for quite a long time. She was staring at Charlie and trying to understand what had just happened. Charlie turned and looked back at her with his usual smirk on his face. Unknown to her, Lydia had just experienced, the first sign.

It was an intensive 21-week course at the FBI Academy in order to become an FBI agent and Tom was glad that he had only three more weeks left. Lydia approached him as he was taking his jacket off.

"They kept you late again?" she asked

"Yes. We had to review a few security protocols and safety stuff."

"Hungry?"

"No honey. I grabbed something to eat before I came home." Tom answered her

"Well, don't make it a habit. I don't want to end up with an old, fat, flabby husband" said Lydia jokingly.

"Don't worry babe. I won't. The fat and flabby I can control; I don't know about the old part."

Lydia put both of her warm palms on Tom's face and asked him. "Do you want a drink?"

"Yes. That would be relaxing." He said as he took off his suit.

"Rum and coke?" she inquired

"With two cherries and a slice of lime, please." replied Tom

Five minutes later Lydia came with two tall glasses. "One for you, one for me" Lydia said handling Tom his rum and coke with two cherries and a slice of lime. Lydia sat on a beige color wingback chair that was placed on a corner of Tom's office.

"And how was your day honey?" Tom asked.

"Busy, doing chores around the house. Talked to mom and dad, and Lily"

"How is she doing?"

"Good considering the situation. But she is still losing a lot of her hair. Poor Lily. That chemotherapy is draining her spirit" Lydia said shaking her head from side to side and taking a sip of her drink.

"She is a strong woman. I know she will pull through" Tom assured Lydia.

"Then, today something strange happened in Charlie's room"

"What do you mean strange?" he asked anxiously.

"Well, I caught him staring at Mayra by her parent's pool, and I don't know, it was as if he was in a trance. He didn't even answer or acknowledge me."

"Come on babe. He is a young boy. Looking at girls is a normal thing. He may be autistic but he is still growing as a man. His hormones are going crazy, you know?"

"I understand, but that was not what was strange about the whole thing" said Lydia.

"What do you mean?" Tom asked taking a big gulp of his drink and giving Lydia a surprised look.

"Well, when I went to see what he was looking at, I covered his eyes like this" Lydia started as she gestured with her hands. "Then, all of a sudden I felt this cold feeling on my body and my eyes got really heavy. The next thing I remember, I was sitting on the edge of his bed staring at him."

"Did he say anything to you?"

"No. He just sat there staring at Mayra"

"And for how long this lasted?"

"Maybe five, eight minutes. I don't really know" Lydia said as she ran her fingers around the rim of the tall glass looking down at her drink.

"Do you feel ok now? Do you want me to call Dr. Brown tomorrow?" He approached Lydia and lifted her chin. "You have been stressed out lately, you should rest" he explained to Lydia.

"Maybe, maybe that's it" Lydia replied

"I can still call Doctor Brown. Maybe he will be able to see you day after tomorrow" Tom counseled.

"No honey that's ok. It must be the stress, that's all." Lydia answered.

Tom squeezed both her hands giving her assurance that he was there for her. Lydia looked back at him; her mouth slightly open shaking her head slightly.

"What Lydia, something else happened?" Tom asked now attentively.

"I may… she started "have said something…"

"To Charlie, did you say something mean to him?"

"No! Not like that. I mean, I felt like I was in some kind of daze, or trance myself. I felt that my lips were moving but I do not remember what I said" explained Lydia.

"Lydia, this is starting to sound really strange. And you said Charlie did not say anything to you."

"Nope. Nothing. He was just staring at that little tramp."

"Now, now…no need for name calling…"

"But it's the truth!" Lydia exclaimed. "That little tramp knew that he was staring at her. She was opening her legs like this" said Lydia imitating Myra's movements. "Licking her lips and smothering herself with sun tan lotion. She wanted to make sure Charlie stared at her."

"Aaaahhh! That little bitch!" Lydia finished explaining herself.

She continued shaking her head as Tom slump on his office chair and continued sipping his beloved rum and coke drink.

"Like I said earlier honey, they are kids. And young kids act idiotic sometimes"

"But I do not want our son to be mentally raped" replied Lydia

Tom started laughing "Come on Lydia. Mentally raped? Ha, ha, ha!"

"You may laugh now, but deep inside you know I'm right. Can you do something? Arrest her for indecent exposure? After all, you are an FBI agent." countered Lydia.

"Not yet. Indecent exposure, to Charlie?" Tom replied.

Lydia put her glass down and grabbed her head with both hands. "I bet you think I am going crazy, don't you?"

"No, I do not, Lydia."

Lydia got up from the wingback chair and asked Tom. "Are you finished with your drink?"

"No. I still have a few drops left" Tom answered her.

"I am going to bed. It's been a strange day for me"

"I heard…" said Tom softly

Before leaving his office he gently grabbed her right arm. "You know I love you right?"

"I know honey. I love you too. If this strange feeling happens again, I will call Doctor Brown myself. Good night honey."

"Good night babe"

Tom had not seen her so confused and preoccupied before. He attentively watched her as she was leaving his office, admiring her beautiful body just as he had admired it many years before, that day they met at the library. But Tom was not aware of one simple fact. And that was that Lydia had experienced her first sign.

2

The next morning Tom woke up at six, he was in a hurry since the drive to the Academy took almost forty five minutes to make. Their neighborhood was just outside Fredericksburg and the morning commute on Interstate 95 was at times brutal. Forty minutes later he was ready to go. Lydia was still sleeping as well as Charlie. He quietly stepped out of the front door and into the Toyota Prius. He thought it was the ugliest car in the world but Lydia had convinced him two years ago that the purchase would be worth it. They would save a ton of money on gas plus Toyota was a very reliable brand, she had told him. Tom drove on Interstate 95 north and almost exactly forty five minutes later he saw the sign; *Quantico Marine Corps Base.* He quickly exited and a few miles later he was at the sprawling 547 acre FBI Academy complex. He was about to enter the brown colored building when his classmate Darren Johnson ran up to him.

"Hey Tom, how is going?" he asked.

"Good Darren. And you?" replied Tom as they walked side by side.

"Great. Had a good weekend family get together, went hiking then went to see a movie. Are you ready for another day in paradise?"

"I am as ready as I am going to be. Hey, do you know where is today's morning briefing?" Tom asked looking around.

"I think is going to be in room 36A today."

"Thanks Darren you are a savior."

"You want to grab a beer after we are done today?"

"Sure. Sounds good Darren." Tom replied.

"Few more weeks buddy, and we will graduate." Darren answered back.

"Can't wait..." replied Tom giving him a thumbs up.

He had met Darren the second week of training at the Academy. Although some of his colleagues considered Darren to be a smart aleck Tom had connected and sympathized with the man. The first day he met Darren he started to tell him right away all about his life. How he had jumped two grades in high school. How he had started college at the young age of sixteen. His high IQ numbers, and his love for astronomy and the search for new stars. He was short, kind of chubby, with curly, light blonde hair and a boyish face. At first Tom thought he would not last a week doing the demanding physical training required from the new trainees. But Darren surprised everyone after he was one of the first five agents in training to finish the five mile run. He respected him not only for that but also for being a genius when it came to the intelligence world, and for being a very helpful friend. It was as if Tom was the only friend he had found at the Academy. They both had decided to concentrate training on being FBI Analysts and Darren would help him anytime he needed. As they got near room 36A a tall man in his mid sixties approached them. It was their supervisor and Lead Trainer Dolan Domenico, or as some nicknamed him around the Academy, 'Big D' because of his big six foot five inch frame. He had a slight resemblance to actor Liam Neeson. He had served as an Army Ranger in Vietnam and retired as a Colonel after twenty five years of service and afterwards decided to join the FBI as an agent in training himself. He wore a three inch scar on his left temple right above his eyebrow courtesy of the North Vietnamese. One of his soldiers had stepped on a landmine killing him instantly and taking another one while they were in a recon mission in 1968. A small piece of shrapnel had embedded on his left temple. Not deep enough to cause brain injury but enough to leave him scarred for life. A few years before, at the tender age of sixty two, his superiors had tried to force him into retiring but essentially he had told them to go screw themselves. He didn't want to hear it. He said he was not ready to retire as his mission was to train more FBI agents to protect and serve his country. When his bosses pressed the retirement issue further he then threatened all of them with an age discrimination lawsuit. He was ready to sue the Academy, the FBI Director, all of his superiors and even the United States President himself. He caused such a stir that his bosses decided to keep him on his post and even gave him a raise in salary instead. After all he was a valuable asset for the Academy. Big D waved to Tom and gave him a hand signal to come over towards him.

"Tom, Darren, can you both come over please?" he asked in a raspy voice.

"Well, good morning Mr. Domenico." Tom said respectfully.

"Good morning sir!" Darren answered him standing at ease.

"I want to show you gentlemen something" Domenico replied.

"Sir, what about the morning briefing?" Darren asked.

"You have been excused." Domenico quickly replied to Darren.

"And our morning notes, sir?"

"Don't worry about your notes Mr. Johnson. I already talked to your morning instructor."

Tom stood quietly, raised his eyebrows and gave a glance to Darren. 'Big D' started walking ahead of them as both Tom and Darren double stepped to catch up to him. They entered a hallway on the left, a big sign above them in gold letters read: *FBI Directorate of Intelligence.* Two huge rooms stood side to side with thick windows about seven feet tall. You could see some of the action going on, people talking to each other, others walking, some typing on the keyboards, but no sound whatsoever. The rooms were completely soundproof. They reached a locked metal door with a security badge swiping system. A sign on the door clearly stated: *Entrance strictly limited to one person at a time. Please swipe your security badge to enter.* Dolan Domenico swiped his badge, got a green light and a loud click was heard. He immediately pushed down the thick door handle and entered the room first. Darren and Tom followed him after each swiped their own security badges. The big room was now noisy with people mingling, chatting, and a lot of clicking from the computer keyboards. About twenty odd shaped desks were scattered around, each with three or four computer monitors and others with three or four keyboards. Above them were two screens at least eighty inches in size and even a bigger one in the middle. One of the eighty inch screens was split into two views, one showing a detailed map of Iran, the other one showing the map of Russia. They came in front of a smaller room with a sign that said *Intel Room 3*. It had the same badge security system as the main room door.

"Agent in training Winston, agent in training Johnson, please sit down." Domenico told them after they all entered the room.

He then closed the door behind him.

Tom and Darren selected two chairs from the long conference table in the Intel room. Another eighty inch screen was in front of them. Dolan started the conversation with "for your information this private briefing is classified Top Secret SKRO, Special Knowledge Required Only." Domenico then turned on the large screen. It was split into two, each showing a man's face.

"AIT Winston, AIT Johnson, do any of you recognize these faces?" he asked them.

"The one on the left is Russian President Nikolai Perchenko. Don't recognize the one on the right" replied Tom.

"Same here sir." Darren acknowledged "Don't know the guy on the right".

"Well, you are both right about the man on the left screen. He is Russia's newly elected President Perchenko. The man on the right is Ecuador's President Eduardo Amador Melancón, himself also recently elected about three months ago as Ecuador's new leader. Since being elected Mr. Melancón has decided to rule Ecuador in the same way as his beloved idol Chavez from Venezuela with a right wing socialist fist. Intelligence that we have gathered tells us that he and

President Perchenko have become close friends. Perchenko has visited Ecuador at least four times since Melancón took over the small South American country. But the most perplexed information we have gathered is that both of them have also visited and toured the Galapagos group of islands, right here" Domenico said pointing with the computer mouse to a map of the islands now on the screen "about five hundred sixty three miles west of the coast of Ecuador to which they belong."

"Galapagos; isn't those the islands where Charles Darwin studied his species?" asked Darren curiously.

"Yes they are AIT Johnson" Dolan replied.

Dolan Domenico continued with the briefing. "Further intelligence we have collected shows that Ecuadorian and Russian military units have performed at least three military exercises during the past three months around the archipelago and more are in planning."

"Why the interest on the part of the Russians, sir?" asked Tom.

"Glad you asked Mr. Winston." Dolan started as he zoomed back on the South American continent using his computer mouse. "Gentlemen, after collecting intelligence from different sources we strongly believe President Perchenko have expressed interest in the control of the Galapagos Islands for two reasons. First, these islands are close to the most traveled commerce causeway in the world, The Panama Canal, which they could disrupt. But the second reason is the most sinister" he added.

"And what is that, sir?" asked Darren now leaning forward in his chair and waiting anxiously for Domenico to answer him.

"We believe Mr. Perchenko plans to bring the latest Russian mobile ballistic missile to these islands."

After Domenico finished this sentence Tom got his attention also and leaned forward on his chair, covering his mouth in awe with his right hand.

"Is he that daring sir…Mr. Perchenko?" asked Darren.

"We believe so. My personal opinion, I think he is a lunatic, willing to test not only us but our allies. Plus, he has found on President

Melancón a good ally who himself is willing to spread his socialist idealism throughout South America."

"How far are those islands from the western United States?" asked Tom.

"Less than three thousand miles from Los Angeles. Not only that but we also found that they may want to bring the SS-45 Galaxy. This is their stealth ballistic missile with very low heat emitting engines, almost undetectable. It can carry up to fifteen warheads, with a maximum range of five thousand miles. Enough to cover the entire western United States."

"Sir, have we been able to track one during testing?"

"No Mr. Winston. We have tried every chance without much success. Out of six lunches inside Russia we were able to track one of them for less than two minutes."

Tom was still leaning forward on his chair while Darren was now staring at the South American continent map, with both of his hands in praying mode.

"The Russian military has appropriately nicknamed their latest toy *prizrak,* meaning The Ghost."

"Excuse me sir, but, why are you telling us all this?" asked Tom reluctantly.

"Well, as you can tell this is top priority, and I want my best Intelligence Analysts working on this."

"Bur sir, with all due respect" Darren started "we are still in training at the Academy."

"I have been watching both of you Mr. Johnson and you two are my top students on our Intelligence Training Unit right now. You speak fluent Russian while Tom is a linguistic expert in Spanish. I strongly believe both of you will be an asset to this mission and you two make a great team."

There was a long pause after Domenico finished as Tom and Darren tried to digest all the information Domenico had dropped on them. Tom leaned back in his chair and asked,

"What do you want us to do sir?"

Dolan Domenico closed his briefing with this note for Tom and Darren.

"Gentlemen, as you can well see from the presentation I have given you we are probably on the verge of a new missile crisis not seen since the Kennedy Presidency. We must do whatever is within our powers to prevent Mr. Perchenko from bringing his Ghosts ICBM missiles to the Galapagos Islands. I want you to use all of your available resources, all that you have learned here, use all your intelligence contacts, and do whatever is necessary to stop this lunatic Perchenko. We want to know everything Perchenko and Melancón are up to. I want both of you to *read their minds*." Domenico concluded.

"We will do everything that is possible sir" Tom said.

"And remember, this was a TS Special Knowledge Required Only briefing. No word on anything we have discussed here. No even to your family members, friends or colleagues here at the FBI Academy. Is that clear?" Domenico emphasized.

"Yes sir!" Tom and Darren replied.

"And if you do, and take my word, I will find out, I'll come after you myself and strangle you with my own two hands" Dolan said looking straight at Darren this time.

AIT Darren Johnson swallowed hard and loosened his shirt collar.

Dolan Domenico then hit Darren slightly on his right shoulder with his fist and told him "I am just fucking with you son…relax. Now, both of you get out of here and get to your next class."

Later that evening AIT Tom Winston and AIT Darren Johnson met outside the main complex building of the FBI Academy.

"What a day Tom. Can you believe that private briefing this morning with Domenico?"

"Yes I do Darren. You know, everything has changed in our country since nine eleven. We keep our friends close, our enemies… closer."

"Well, ready for that beer?" Darren asked him.

"I sure am" Tom answered "I'll drive."

The Second Sign

"Charlie!" Lydia said loudly from the front door of their home. "Come on babe, I do not want to miss the sale at Macy's this morning."

It was getting close to Charlie's 13th birthday and for Lydia it would be a very special one. The time her son would turn into a teenager, no longer a baby or toddler but a teenager with special needs. She had decided first to stop at the neighborhood grocery store where she could buy something special to cook for dinner. She climbed into the dark blue Honda Odyssey van and buckled Charlie to the backseat. Charlie sat there, as always, looking outside without saying a word. Lydia knew he would not speak to her unless spoken to him first. She always needed to start the conversation first, or he would just stay in his own private world. Lydia wanted so badly to get inside his head, his likes, his dislikes, his hobbies, what he wanted to be when he would get older, what he wanted to study. He had tried in many occasions to no avail. The more she tried the more he pulled away from her. Lydia glanced at Charlie thru the rearview mirror.

"Are you ok honey?" she asked him

"Yes mom. OK" Charlie replied

"Do you like going shopping with mom, Charlie?"

"Yes, going shopping with mom" he said still staring outside.

Lydia could not contain her curiosity any longer. She asked him. "Charlie," she asked clearing her throat and then glancing at him on the rear view mirror again. "Do you like looking at…girls?"

Charlie then gave Lydia that devilish smile without answering her question.

"Do you like looking at Mayra?" she asked again.

Not a word from Charlie but his unique smirk.

"Ok, let's drop the subject then since obviously we are not making any progress with this conversation."

"We are going shopping now, are we going shopping mom, is mom shopping now?" he started saying.

"Yes Charlie. Here we are. We are getting some groceries first"

She liked visiting the small mom and pops markets to purchase the food for the family. She hated those gigantic supermarkets where they sold everything from tires to so called fresh fish. And the combination of the smell from both was not too appetizing either. She parked in front of the Trader Joe's food market, picked up a shopping cart and holding Charlie by the hand they entered the store. Fresh flowers in all colors, sizes and smells always greeted the customers. Lydia loved it so much that at times she would stand by the front entrance, her eyes closed, just letting her sense of smell catch all the different aromas from those fresh cut flowers. At times she would stand there for so long with Charlie that some shoppers thought she was delusional. She did not care what they thought. As far as she knew the smell was free and she was going to enjoy it. She picked up two boxes of organic cereal, apples, some pears, and four of those wraps that she and Tom liked so much.

"Charlie, do you want cranberry juice?" she asked him.

"Yes mom. Cranberry juice, yes. Cranberry juice mom" he said.

As she was turning into the next aisle a friend from her yoga class almost bumped into her cart.

"Lydia! How are you doing? Nice to see you again" she greeted her.

"Hey, hello Tracy. Nice seeing you too"

"And hello young man. You must be Charlie" she said looking at him. Charlie did not answer her back. He stared at her for a few seconds then looked away.

"Sorry Tracy. He does not talk much" replied Lydia. Then she turned to Charlie. "Charlie, this is my friend Tracy. We take yoga classes together".

"Yes. Hello" Charlie said to her friend Tracy.

"It's ok. I understand Lydia. No apologies are necessary."

"He is growing so fast. He will be a teenager soon" Lydia responded caressing his hair.

"Is that so?" Tracy replied.

"Yes, he will be thirteen in a couple of months. We are planning a very special birthday party for the occasion. You and your family should come"

"That sounds great Lydia. Just let me know when."

Charlie pulled Lydia's hand. "Let's go shopping mom, let's go shopping, are we going shopping mom?" He was now getting anxious, moving his head from side to side. All of a sudden, he stopped and stared right at Lydia's friend Tracy. He then squeezed Lydia's hand. Lydia suddenly felt that feeling again she had experienced earlier at Charlie's room. A cold feeling all over her body overwhelmed her, her eyes got really heavy as if in a trance. With her other hand she grabbed the handle on the shopping cart.

"Lydia, are you ok? Lydia? Lydia?" Tracy kept asking.

Lydia felt her lips moving against her will again, saying something, but could not hear herself. But Tracy could. Mesmerized, Tracy heard clearly what she was saying;

"Poor Lydia, feel so sorry for her! Almost always alone to raise this kid. Her husband is never there, for God's sake! I don't know how they make it. At least he will be earning more money after he graduates. Hope he is not cheating on her." After saying these words she felt dizzy, and grabbed the cart's handle with both hands before her legs gave up on her.

"Lydia! Oh my God!" Tracy screamed as she grabbed her around her waist. Immediately one of the employees at Trader Joe's came over after she heard Tracy's screams. Lydia was just standing there, puzzled, and with Tracy and about ten other patrons at the store staring at her and Charlie.

"Lady, are you alright? Do you want me to call the medics?" the employee of the market said to her.

"Do we have a doctor here!?" she yelled.

"No. no!" Lydia started saying to her. "I'm ok. Just a little bit tired, that's all. Have not been eating well lately"

"Are you sure Lydia? Do you want me to drive you home?" Tracy offered.

"I am sure. No need"

"Miss, if you need any help, don't hesitate to call one of us" the employee said.

"Really appreciate it. Thank you." Lydia assured her.

Charlie stared at the floor. "Mom is shopping, mom is shopping"

Lydia grabbed him by the hand. "Let's go honey. Let's go home. Dad is waiting."

Lydia exited the market store quickly leaving the cart with all the food items inside of it. She secured Charlie to the car seat. She sat on the driver's seat of her Honda van and slumped her forehead on the steering wheel. She could not believe it, it had happened again. The same feelings she had felt that day when she was at Charlie's room. She could not tell Tom as she did not want him to worry about her even more. Suddenly she jumped from the seat as she heard a knock on the window and rolled it down. It was Tracy again.

"Feeling better, Lydia?" she asked concerned

"Yes, I am Tracy. Thanks for your concern. We will be heading back home soon." Lydia assured her.

"If you need anything call me ok?" Tracy said gesturing with her hand.

"I will. Thanks again Tracy"

Tracy started walking back to the Trader Joe's. She glanced twice back at Lydia and Charlie with a strange, surprised look on her face. Lydia had a feeling that Tracy was not going to be present for Charlie's thirteenth birthday.

That night Lydia acted as if nothing had happened that day. She did not confer anything to Tom other than telling him that she and Charlie had gone to the stores. Getting him worried with her problems was the last thing on her mind especially when he was getting closer to his graduation from the FBI Academy. She wanted him to be one hundred percent concentrated on his training at the Academy and pursuing the dream he had work for so hard. Tom and Lydia went to bed after a quiet, relaxing, and uneventful night. But unbeknown to them, earlier that day, Lydia had encountered a second sign.

The next morning Lydia got up early from bed right after Tom had left to the Academy. She was still trying to comprehend what had happened to her the day before at the market. She really started to worry. Where the symptoms she was experiencing related to a dreadful disease? Her mother had succumbed to cancer at the age of only forty eight and her older sister Lily was now suffering from the same awful disease and taking chemotherapy in order to slow it down. She was distraught that the symptoms she was having were somehow related to the beginning of cancer. But for some oddball reason she was also convinced that it was something else, something different affecting her. She stared at herself on the bathroom mirror. She slowly took all of her clothes off and started to examine her body for any unusual marks. She checked her breasts, under her arms, chest, face, under her tongue, and buttocks. But she did not find anything unusual. She then took a quick shower and got dressed. She went into Tom's office and turned on his computer, logged in, and opened the Google search page. After staring at the cursor for what it seemed like a lifetime, she started typing words that she hoped would give her an answer for her strange symptoms. She typed *sleep disorders, sleepwalking, dreams, mental illness, schizophrenia,* and many other terms she thought her illness would be related to. But none of them provided her with the answers she was looking for. She had been at the computer for almost two hours researching. Frustrated, she rubbed her eyes, getting nowhere with these. She was about to get up from the chair when she decided to search using a combination of two words. Specific words came to her mind. After typing them about seven different links popped up on the computer screen. Lydia started reading attentively each article that was related to those two words she had typed. Could this be the answer she was looking for? *'Is this related to what is happening to me?'* she asked herself. *'If I tell Tom he will think I am crazy'.* She needed to convince Tom that what was happening to her was real, although it would sound totally unbelievable. When she finished reading the last article she had been in front of the computer screen for almost four hours. Lydia could not wait to show Tom what her research had produced.

That evening as soon as they were done with dinner Lydia called Tom to his office.

"Tom, honey. I got something to show you" she said to him handing him about ten printed pages.

"Oh, and what is this?" Tom asked

"Tom, I took it upon myself to try to find an answer for what it's been happening to me."

"What do you mean *happening,* Lydia? Has it happened more than once then?"

"Yes, Tom. I…didn't want to tell you. I didn't want to bother you now especially that you are so close to your graduation from The Academy" she tried to explain to Tom.

"But honey" he started touching her hair, then pulled her closer to him. "I want you to tell me everything that ails you, bothers you, and worries you. Do you understand? I am your husband, and that is why I am here, ok?" Lydia nodded her head to let Tom know she agreed with him.

"So, when and where did it happen again?" Tom asked her.

"Yesterday, at the market store" she said reluctantly.

"What exactly happened?"

"Well, actually, the same symptoms I felt the first time I was inside Charlie's bedroom."

"Did anyone try to help you there at the store?"

"Yes. But I told them not to bother. I just told them that I had not been eating well lately."

"That's it Lydia! I'm calling Dr. Brown tomorrow and I will go with you. We can leave Charlie with your mother" Tom answered her affirmatively.

"No Tom, please! I do not want to see any doctors, not yet" she answered back.

"And why not?" Tom replied with an upset tone in his voice.

"Because…because I do not think it has to do anything with my health."

"Oh…are you trying to diagnose yourself now?" he asked.

"Please Tom. I want you to read these articles I printed earlier" she said to Tom pointing to the small stack of about ten printed pages she handed him before. Tom gave a long stare to Lydia, picked up the first page and started to read. He then read the second page and the third while Lydia sat quietly on the corner wingback chair. After reading the fourth page Tom rendered his opinion.

"Honey, this seems to have more to do with Charlie than with the problems you are experiencing."

"I know" answered Lydia.

"You know. What do you mean by that?"

"I get the sense that…somehow it involves me too, Tom."

"In what way, Lydia?"

"Like I told you. I have a sense that what I am experiencing has something to do with this" Lydia responded pointing towards the printed papers once again. Tom let out a long sigh, tilted his head back, and slowly back forward. With his feet he dragged the office chair towards Lydia's corner. He put both of his hands on Lydia's thighs.

"Ok honey. You must understand my reluctance here. I would need more; let's say, proof that what you printed from some website has something to do with the experiences that you have encountered lately" he tried to explain to her.

"Promise me you will read all ten pages before you make your mind."

Tom nodded his head yes and clasped her right hand. "I promise babe I will. I will read all ten pages, ok?"

"Thank you dear" Lydia said with a relief on her voice now. "And for not thinking I am crazy."

"Yes, I know you are crazy. Crazy for me, that is…" Lydia gave Tom a quick kiss.

"Thank you my love" she said back. "Now, get on with reading" she added.

While Lydia walked back towards the stairs she glanced back twice at Tom to see if he really was going to keep his promise. She stopped by the first step and quietly peeked at Tom while he read. He was now attentively reading the other pages. After reading the last one she saw Tom shaking his head in awe. "Oh my God!" Tom exclaimed. "Is this possible?" Tom asked himself as he stacked the papers neatly on top of his desk. On the papers Lydia had printed he could clearly see the search terms that his worried wife had input into the computer. The two words were *autism* and *telepathic powers*. Still hiding by the stairs like a little kid running away from her father's belt Lydia whispered to herself "Yes it is Tom. Yes it is!"

3

"God damned it!" Dolan yelled as he and two of his assistants watched the CNN channel. Wolf Blitzer was reporting from his new hour long show World Watch.

"And as we have been reporting all day long" Wolf Blitzer started "we are following breaking news concerning some unusual Russian Navy exercises close to the coast of the country of Ecuador. We now have our defense department correspondent Barbara Starr with us to find out more about the latest developments. Barbara?"

"Hello, Wolf."

"Barbara, can you tell us the latest developments regarding these Russian ships off the coast of Ecuador?"

"Yes, Wolf. Our sources from the Defense department tells us that they are closely following unusual activity of what it looks like Russian Navy exercises between the coast of Ecuador and the Galapagos Islands. Our source also tells us that they think that the Ecuadorian Navy may also be involved in these military exercises. They say they are closely monitoring the situation as it develops and that the Defense Department has briefed the President already about these developments. Wolf?"

"You bring a good point Barbara, and that is that these exercises would have to have the blessing of the Ecuadorian government as it seems that they are already involved in exercises with the Russian Navy. Any word from the White House about that Barbara?" Wolf asked.

"No. They are keeping pretty quiet about it, and as they told us earlier Secretary of Defense Donovan and the Joints Chiefs have already briefed the President concerning these alarming news."

"Barbara, I was reading earlier about these islands and they have a pretty interesting story. I read that at one time the United States even considered purchasing the archipelago from the Ecuadorian government in the early 1900's. Have you heard anything about this?"

"That is correct, Wolf. During the early 1900's and up to the 1930's the United States seriously considered buying the group of islands from then cash strapped Ecuador. The United States wanted to purchase the same in order to protect the Panama Canal and even during World War II the Ecuadorian government authorized the establishment of a US Navy base on one of the archipelago islands."

"Barbara, can you tell us, what is the main concern from the Defense Department regarding Russian ships on this part of the world?"

"Well Wolf. They are not saying much except for the fact that they are continuing checking the situation. But as we take a look at the map of South America there is no question about the strategic location of these islands that are less than three thousand miles from the western coast of the United States. Wolf?"

"Thank you Barbara for these latest news…" Dolan turned the television off as another of his assistants peeked his head into his office.

"Dolan, Deputy Secretary Mallory is not happy" he told Dolan.

"That's all I need. That little shit!" he yelled back. "I'll deal with him later."

He waved him to go away and then dialed Tom Winston's cell number.

"Hello?" Tom answered on the other line.

"Mr. Winston, have you watched the news today?" he asked him.

"Oh…Mr. Domenico. Yes sir, I have."

"Well, if you have, then get your ass in my office in twenty" he said in his raspy voice. "I already called your partner Johnson."

Thomas L. Winston arrived at Domenico's office exactly twenty two minutes after the call. When he entered Domenico's office Darren Johnson was already there. He was sitting in front of the conference table, his eyes staring at it, with his chin down and with his arms crossed in front of his chest as if he had been reprimanded by his school teacher.

"Well hello Mr. Winston. Glad you could join us" Domenico greeted him as he entered the office. "I am sure you both know why I called you here."

"The CNN report I am guessing" Darren said.

"That is correct AIT Johnson. About a week ago I gave you both a highly classified briefing regarding the moves by the Russian Navy by the coast of Ecuador. Then today, the Communist News Network happens to be reporting about the same thing. I take it it's hard to believe it is just coincidence, gentlemen."

"Sir, you don't think that one of us…" Tom started saying with an ambushed look "talked to the network, do you?"

Dolan stood straight, his fists locked and firmly planted by his waist, as if ready to brief his troops before going to battle.

"I hope neither of you did Mr. Winston. And if I find out otherwise that will be the end of your careers as Special FBI Agents. Not only that but I will make sure that both of you end up in Leavenworth making little rocks out of big ones for the rest of your natural lives!" Dolan said almost screaming by the end of his sentence.

"Sir, I give you my word that neither I nor Darren talked to anyone regarding the briefing you gave us, sir." Tom replied looking straight at Dolan.

"I got the same answer from your partner here" said Dolan pointing at Darren who was now rocking on his chair. "I believe you both, but God forgive me if I find out otherwise. Do you both got me?"

"Yes sir!" answered Darren

"Yes sir!" repeated Tom

"Any of you have anything new to report regarding Perchenko or President Melancón?"

"Sir, I have contacted my assets in Ecuador but have not been able to obtain any specifics. Pretty quiet and dry down there."

"Same here sir. Many of my contacts in Moscow are either unaware of what is going on or they have been threaten not to say anything. I'll keep digging though" Tom replied.

"Good. Keep searching. We need to find what they are up to and what their next move is. By the way I was going to show you…" Dolan started, but before he could complete his thought a man of short stature burst into the office unannounced.

"Mr. Domenico. Are you giving another one of your briefings?" Deputy Secretary of Defense Roy Mallory asked.

"No sir. Just conferring with my two top candidates Mr. Winston and Mr…"

"Yes. Mr. Johnson, correct?" he interrupted.

Deputy Secretary of Defense Roy Mallory had been closely following the news all throughout the day and had stayed close by, waiting and circling like a shark before attacking his next victim. He was short, five feet four inches tall, and very well dressed. He dressed only in expensive handmade suits and always wore his crocodile skin boots. Everyone inside the office could smell and almost choke from the strong cologne he showered himself with. Dolan himself and his staff had nicknamed him "Napo Roy" because of his small physique and strong Napoleonic Complex. At the age of forty two he was the youngest person to ever occupy this post.

"Do you know who I am?" he asked turning towards Tom and Darren. Darren was now standing at attention.

"Yes sir we do" Tom answered for both of them.

Roy Mallory was now picking small pieces of lint from his handmade suit with his perfectly manicured fingers. "This office could use a good cleaning" he said. "Since you know who I am I will be brief and to the point then. I want both of you trainees to turn into my office any documents, briefings, photos, disks, or anything that has to do with the Ecuadorian and Russian situation."

"But sir," Darren started "Mr. Domenico said…" Roy Mallory interrupted once again.

"I know that Mr. Domenico briefed you concerning the volatile situation off the coast of Ecuador. But let's make this perfectly clear AIT Johnson" he pointed to Dolan "Mr. Domenico works for me, do you understand?"

"I…understand clearly sir" Darren replied.

"And how is the world treating you Mr. Domenico?" he asked turning towards Dolan.

"Very well sir. Trying my best to do my job, mister secretary."

"Thinking about retiring yet, Mr. Domenico?"

"No, Mr. Secretary. Haven't even crossed my mind."

"Hmmm…you are now almost…"

"I know what my age is sir. No need to remind me." Dolan interrupted his sentence

Roy Mallory put his manicured hands inside the soft pockets of his perfectly ironed trousers as he paced around the office. Tom and Darren could now feel the tension between these two and nervously looked at each other. Deputy Secretary of Defense Mallory broke the ice after almost two minutes of silence. Dolan was an imposing figure over Roy Mallory and Roy clearly wanted all of them to know who was in charge.

"Dolan, can I call you Dolan?" he asked.

"No sir." Dolan quickly replied.

"Hmmm…very well, mister Domenico. I want to make sure that your trainees Johnson and Winston clearly understand that they are not part of this mission as of today. All intelligence reports are to go directly to my office. Your Agents In Training are out of the loop. Understand?"

"Yes sir. Understood."

"I do not want any more leaks to the media concerning the Perchenko and the Russian Navy exercises off the coast of Ecuador.

And anyone that violates this policy will be dealt with and will answer directly to me."

"I assure you sir. AIT's Winston and Johnson had nothing to do with it." Dolan replied.

Roy Mallory slowly walked towards Dolan Domenico until he was only a few inches in front of him. He then looked up to Dolan's face.

"I know you care about your trainees, Mr. Domenico. But this is not the Army anymore. These are not your soldiers. They are simply FBI Cadets, Agents In Training, AIT's. And your boss answers to me, so, that makes me YOUR boss, doesn't it?" Dolan's face was now turning red with anger.

"I guess you are sir."

"You guess?" Roy started with a hint of disbelief on his face "are you trying to be a smartass, mister Domenico?"

"No sir!" Dolan answered right away.

"Good then." Roy said starting to pick again at his suit. "Let's go guys, we have work to do" he said motioning to his entourage that had been standing by the door. Before making an exit Mallory opened the door slightly and stuck his head back into Dolan's office.

"Oh… and Domenico. If I was you I would be seriously thinking about a nice place to retire soon. Good afternoon gentlemen." He then slammed the door behind him.

After a few more minutes of silence that seem like an eternity for Darren he asked,

"Are we done here sir? Do we turn in everything to the secretary?"

"You will do no such thing!" Dolan responded in anger.

"But sir, you heard him."

"I heard what he said, Mr. Johnson. God damned it, I may be old but my fucking hearing is just fine!" he fired back.

"But after all sir, he is still the Deputy Secretary of Defense." Tom injected. "We will be in serious trouble if we do not…"

"Don't worry mister Winston. I would not put your careers in peril. But believe me when I tell you both. That little cocksucker ain't got nothin on me. The only reason he was appointed to his position is because of his daddy. He has been a long time chairman of the Intelligence Committee and a well respected senator in Washington. Fucking politicians. Even secretary Donovan despises him" he finished shaking his head.

Startled at what they just had witnessed Darren asked "Where do we go from here sir?"

"We stay the course son. Our plans have not changed. I want to be the first to know about Perchenko's and Melancón's plans. And the sooner we know the better."

He stared out his office window as the black Chevy Suburban carrying Deputy Secretary of Defense Roy Mallory sped away. His train of thought was broken by the sound of a phone ring.

"It's my wife sir. May I?" asked Tom

"Sure, go ahead Mr. Winston" replied Dolan

It was Lydia on the phone and she was crying uncontrollably.

"Honey, what's wrong?" Tom asked her "Something happen? Are you alright?"

"Tom," she started to say, but her sobbing and crying got worse. "Oh my God, Tom!"

"Lydia, honey, are you hurt? What is going on?" Tom asked anxiously. The phone line went quiet for a few seconds. Tom could hear Lydia's deep sobbing breaths on the line. Finally she composed herself.

"I am fine Tom. It's my sister Lily. Her cancer cells are not responding to treatment and she is in intensive care at Boston Memorial Hospital. The doctors say she may not have long."

The Third Sign

Lydia, along with Charlie, decided to take the first flight to Boston the next day. She had convinced Tom to stay home since his FBI training was coming to an end, and needed to concentrate on his upcoming graduation. The flight took about two hours but Lydia was not able to rest her body, many things went thru her mind. Charlie sat quietly next to her reading the UFC magazine he had gotten from a friend from school. Upon de boarding the airplane they went straight to their hotel room. She opened the hotel room door; she was exhausted, not as much physically, but mentally. She had gone thru the same routine with her mother when she was much younger and really hated the thought of having to visit a hospital again to visit a relative. She dropped the suitcase on the bed, sat on the edge of it, and started to sob loudly. Charlie recognized her suffering and sadness, her mother was crying because of something, she was really sad about something.

"Mom, why are you crying?" Charlie asked her.

"Come here honey. I need to tell you something"

"But why are you crying, mom?" he asked again

"I am going to tell you, come closer to mommy" Lydia said as she pulled him closer to her by pulling on his left arm.

"Do you remember Aunt Lily?" There was a short pause from Charlie before he answered.

"Yes, I know Aunt Lily. She bought me the train set for Christmas, mom".

"Yes! That's her!" Lydia answered joyfully.

Charlie then added "And she came with grandpa for my birthday too".

"Yes she did Charlie. Well…" Lydia cleared her throat twice before offering an explanation of what was about to come. "Aunt Lily, Charlie, is very, very sick. And you and me are going to visit her later today at a hospital here in Boston, ok?" she explained caressing his hair.

"What do you mean?" he asked, his face pouting.

"Honey, Auntie Lily got very sick a long time ago and she has gotten worse in the past few weeks".

"Was it something she ate?" Charlie asked.

"No honey, it was not something she ate. It's just that sometimes… aunts, uncles, and family that we care about very much get really sick because of bad diseases. And, sometimes, no matter how much medicines they take they get sicker, and sicker."

"Is Aunt Lily coming with us when she gets better mom?"

Lydia started to cry again and hugged Charlie tight. "I hope so honey, I hope so." She said to Charlie as she held her son tight on her arms.

"Don't cry mommy, don't cry. We will *talk* with her soon." Charlie responded as he pat his mother's back softly with his small hands.

Boston Memorial Hospital was twenty minutes from their hotel. Lydia and Charlie got out of the taxi and she stood in front of the entrance, hesitant to go thru the front doors of a place where people lots of times come to die. Charlie squeezed her hand and Lydia gave him back a slight smile. They immediately went to the information desk and asked a hospital volunteer for her sister's room number.

"Hello, I am here to visit my sister Lillian Chandler."

"Is the little guy a relative too, Miss?" the desk attendant asked while smiling at Charlie. Charlie smiled back at her.

"Yes, he is her nephew. He is my son."

The hospital volunteer, a lady with silver, almost white hair, in her seventies and with a slight hunch slowly typed Lillian's name into the computer screen. She looked back and forth at the screen and then at Lydia about three times. She then asked "and your name is?"

"My name is Lydia Winston and this is my son Charlie Winston" she answered her.

"Well, Mrs. Winston your sister has been transferred to section six on the third floor, room 206. Just take the elevator here to the third floor; take a left and another attendant will meet you there."

"What do you mean transferred?" Lydia asked surprised.

The old lady with silver hair raised her eyebrows, vacillating to answer her.

"The attendant will meet you upstairs, Mrs. Winston" she said to Lydia.

"Please tell me, it's my sister we are talking about. My only sister!" she begged her for an answer.

The old lady signaled her to come closer towards the counter. She then whispered close to Lydia's face. "It's our...our... hospice section. Sorry dear" she said as she pat Lydia's right hand.

Lydia felt like screaming at the world, felt light headed, but contained herself especially in front of Charlie.

"Thank you so much!" Lydia replied to the old lady.

"May god bless you and your family my dear" she answered back.

Lydia started walking towards the elevators holding Charlie's hand tight while she tried to take some tissues from inside her purse. She was drying her tears when the elevator door opened on the third floor. She took a left as the lady had instructed her and was amazed to see the same old lady already standing at the third floor information help desk. He asked her "how did you…?"

"Got here so fast darling?" she said to Lydia

"Yes, how did you get here before us?"

"That is my sister down there at the main entrance. My twin sister, that is. We get asked the same question many times in a single day. We volunteer here three times a week. Now, how can I help you?"

"I am here to see my sister Lillian Chandler. This is my son Charlie. My name is Lydia Winston."

"Sure my darling. Come, come sit down here. And hello young man, and how old are you?" she asked turning to Charlie.

"I'm sorry…Claudia?" Lydia started saying peeking at her name tag. "He doesn't talk too…"

"I'm almost thirteen" Charlie quickly answered.

"Wow! Thirteen. I remember when I was thirteen. I loved to drink lots of root beer floats back then. Do you like root beer floats, Charlie?" Claudia asked him.

"Yes I do." Charlie said. Claudia then slowly pulled another chair and sat right in front of Charlie. "So, are you coming to visit your auntie with your mom?"

"Yes. My auntie Lily is really sick and we came to visit her today" Charlie responded while staring at the floor and moving his legs back and forth. Suddenly, Charlie looked into Claudia's deep blue eyes.

"And your aunt Lily is going to *talk to you*, isn't she?" asked Claudia.

"Yes she is, and to mommy too."

"Yes she is honey, yes she is" Claudia said as she patted Charlie's hand.

She slowly got her small frame up from the chair and turned to Lydia.

"Darling…" she said to her pointing towards a set of double doors. "You go thru those double doors and ask for Dr. Miller. He will take you to see your sister" Claudia finished with a smile.

"Thank you Claudia"

Lydia was utterly surprised. That was the longest conversation that Charlie had ever had with a stranger. They went thru the double doors, the sign on top read: *Boston Memorial Hospice Wing* and right below it another smaller sign read; "*May the Lord bless you and all families that go thru these doors.*"

Dr. Miller was the only physician/psychiatrist assigned to the Hospice Wing. As soon as he saw Lydia he could see the resemblance in her sister Lillian even after the physical changes caused by her aggressive cancer. He extended his arm to greet Lydia.

"Lillian's sister, I assume?" he said

"Yes I am. My name is Lydia Winston and this is my son Charlie. And you are Doctor Miller, I presume. Nice to meet you doctor" said Lydia shaking his hand. "How is my sister doctor?"

"I will be truthful with you Lydia. Lillian's cancer has stopped responding to chemo treatment. The cancer cells have grown aggressively in the past two weeks and we have tried numerous combinations of medications, even experimental ones, with no avail. She is a strong woman but I am afraid that at this point we have done everything we can for her. I am so sorry, Mrs. Winston."

Lydia nodded her head yes trying to understand that cancer had won the battle with her only sister just as it had won with her mother.

"I understand, doctor. Thanks for doing everything in your power for my sister. How long does she have Doctor Miller?" Lydia asked.

"We are making her as comfortable as we can. In my experience I would say she has three, maybe four weeks at the most" Doctor Miller said.

"Oh my God!" Lydia exclaimed covering her mouth with her left hand and still holding Charlie with the other.

"If there is anything we can do to make your sister more comfortable or your family, please don't hesitate to let me know or any of my staff. We are here to support you and your relatives."

"Thank you doctor. Can I see her now?"

"Sure. Follow me. She is in room 206."

Upon entering room two zero six Lydia could hardly recognize her sister Lily. Her frame had dwindled to about seventy five pounds, her beautiful curly brown hair was gone, her eyes sunk so deeply that they looked as if they were only sockets, but no eyes at all. Tubes were inserted on her nose, a respirator mask was on her face and multiple machines attached to her now diminutive body monitored her oxygen, heart, pulse, and other body functions. She wasn't sure if she wanted to see her like this. Lydia approached the bed slowly and grabbed her sister's hand. Lily's hand was cold, bony, and two intravenous needles were inserted on her now thin skin. Lydia's hand started to shake.

"Lily, can you hear me? I know you cannot talk to me because of all of these machines they have you hooked up to. I just wanted to tell you that I am here with Charlie. He wanted to see you too. Tom could not make it, but he sends you his love. I love you very, very much. Hang in there, sis." He motioned to Charlie to get closer to his aunt. "Charlie, you want to say something to your aunt Lily?"

"Hello, Aunt Lily. I love you and I want you to come with us when you get better" Charlie said.

"Sorry honey. I am sure she can hear you but she cannot talk to us because of her oxygen mask. She is also very weak."

"Yes, she can talk to us, mom."

"I am sorry honey, she can't. She is very fragile and they cannot remove her oxygen mask. I wish we could..." Suddenly, Charlie grabbed Lydia's right hand.

Again, Lydia felt that coldness throughout her body that she had experienced before, and the weird notion of her body and mind transferred to another place. She was holding Charlie's hand tightly. All of a sudden Lydia started talking and spitting out words beyond her control. *'Hi Lydia. I am so happy to see you and Charlie. I love you and Charlie very much. I am so sorry I could not beat this damn disease that has consumed my body. Please sis, do not feel sad for me. Go on with your life Lydia, be happy and love each other more every day. I am going to see mom soon. I will always be with you!'*

Lydia snapped out of it as soon as she let Charlie's hand go. For some odd reason she could now remember most of the words she had said while in the trance. Whose words were those? Where they her sister's Lily? Impossible, as she was completely unable to speak a word!

"I told you she could talk to us, mom" Charlie suddenly said.

"What? What do you mean honey?" Lydia asked puzzled.

"Aunt Lily. She talked to us, just like the old lady said."

"What do you mean Charlie?"

She then remembered the words from Claudia to Charlie while they were waiting by the information desk; *'and your aunt Lily is going to talk to you, isn't she?'*

"Oh my God! How did she know? Charlie, what else did she say to you?" she screamed at him.

"That's all she said, mom" Charlie replied frightened.

"Sorry honey. I didn't mean to scare you. Mom is confused, very confused now."

Lydia took a long look at her dying sister lying on the hospital bed. Her oxygen mask was still on her face. But most of the words she had said before were now so clear she was almost sure were Lily's. She remembered Charlie and Claudia's conversation earlier. Claudia, yes, the old lady volunteer. She needed to talk to her. What had she meant when talking to Charlie? Was she in any way connected with what was happening to her? She needed to know now. She grabbed her sister's hand again.

"Lily, I love you so much. We are all praying for you sis. We will visit you again soon. Daddy called me earlier. He said he will be here sometime this evening." She bent down and kissed her sister on the forehead. "Love you lots, Lily" she said.

When Lydia and Charlie were out on the hallway she waved to a nurse close by.

"Miss, can you help me?" Lydia asked the nurse.

"Yes, what can I do for you?"

"I would like to talk to one of your volunteers, Claudia; I believe is her name, old lady in her seventies?"

"Hmm…I don't recall anyone like that as one of our volunteers, Miss…"

"Winston, Mrs. Winston" Lydia replied.

"I do not believe anyone fits that description but come with me, I will ask in our department."

Lydia and Charlie followed her to the nurses' station where two other nurses were on duty that day. The nurse then called to the other nurses.

"Eileen, Brian, do you know of any volunteer by the name of Claudia? A lady in her seventies?"

"Yes, with silver, almost white hair" Lydia injected.

Both nurses shook their heads no.

"But, I just talked to them today before I visited my sister in room 206."

"Them? Is it more than one then?" one of the nurses asked.

"Yes, they were twin sisters. One was on the main entrance front desk, and the other one was here, on the third floor."

"No, I don't recall seeing any volunteers like that" Eileen responded.

"Me neither" agreed Brian. "But I can call HR. Maybe they know. Give me a few minutes. And your name is?"

"Lydia Winston. I'll wait here with my son." Lydia said while they took a seat on a bench by the hallway. Almost fifteen minutes later nurse Brian finally approached Lydia.

"Mrs. Winston, our Human Resources department says that they have never hired anybody for the hospital with that description. I know it is a stressful time for you and your family. Perhaps you confused them with someone else?"

"No. I know we saw them, and my son did too. Maybe they work in another department, the cafeteria, maybe?" Lydia asked anxiously.

"Mrs. Winston, I've been working here for almost ten years. I have never seen anyone inside this hospital that fits the description you gave us. Less two of them."

Lydia stood up from the bench. "Ok. You are telling me that no one has ever worked at this hospital that even comes close to the persons I described to you?"

"That is what I am telling you Mrs. Winston."

Lydia covered her face with both her hands in disbelief. "It doesn't make any sense. It's crazy!"

"Sorry Mrs. Winston. Anything else we can help you with?" asked nurse Brian.

"No, no. Thanks for checking for me. Come on Charlie. We are going back to the hotel, honey. We really need some rest."

At the hotel later that night Lydia decided to call Tom. She wanted to tell him all about the unusual day but she decided instead to concentrate the conversation on Lily's situation. They talked for about a half hour, and about nine fifteen at night she got Charlie ready for bed. Before giving him a goodnight kiss Lydia decided to give it another try with Charlie.

"Charlie, do you remember talking to the old lady Claudia?"

"Yes, mom. I remember. She was friendly with us."

"Do you remember if she said anything else to you...other than... talking about aunt Lily?"

"No mom. She only told me that auntie Lily was going to *talk* to us" Charlie answered.

"Ok honey. Sorry about all the questions. It should be the other way around."

"Ok mom"

Lydia gave Charlie a kiss on his forehead and lay down on the other bed. She turned her head away from Charlie's bed, her eyes wide open. He then heard Charlie's voice.

"Mom, she was an angel" Charlie said from his bed.

Lydia did not turn to face Charlie. She covered her mouth trying hard not to cry again.

"Mom?" Charlie asked again

"Yes Charlie?" Lydia said still facing away and trying hard not to cry.

"Can we get root beer floats tomorrow?" he asked.

With an astonished look on her face, and halfway sobbing Lydia answered him.

"Yes, honey. We can get root beer floats tomorrow."

4

Lydia and Charlie slept late the following morning. They took a flight home leaving the airport three hours later around eleven thirty in the morning and arrived home where Tom had cooked a welcomed, hearty dinner for them. Tom was anxiously waiting by the driveway as the taxi pulled in front of their house. Lydia and Tom hugged for quite a long time, and then they kissed.

"Hello honey. I missed you a lot" Tom greeted Lydia.

"Me too! I wish you could have been there with me."

"Sorry babe. Getting close to graduation and it's getting crazy at the academy."

"I understand Tom. I want you to be ready when the time comes."

All of a sudden Charlie jumped out of the back of the taxi. He was holding tight to a big cup of root beer float Lydia had just purchased for him.

"Hello buddy. How was your trip Charlie? Want to give dad a hug?" Charlie just ignored him, his eyes fixed on that root beer float. He started drinking from it.

Tom again tried to get his attention. "What do you have there, buddy?"

"My root beer float" Charlie answered him.

"Root beer float? I didn't know you liked root beer floats."

"Claudia wanted me to have one" said Charlie.

"Who? Who is Claudia?" Tom asked him then glancing at Lydia

"I'll explain later Tom" Lydia interrupted.

"Oh, ok." Tom answered as he carried their luggage inside the house

Tom had prepared a very nice dinner for his family. Meat lasagna, Italian tossed green salad, garlic bread, a semi-sweet wine, and tiramisu cake for dessert. Lydia changed quickly into her comfortable bedtime clothes while Charlie stayed inside his room. The sound of Michael Jackson's Thriller song could be heard from his room.

"Charlie, come down to eat honey. Dad made a terrific dinner for us" Lydia yelled from downstairs

"I am not hungry mom" Charlie yelled back, his room door still close.

"Well, I guess that root beer float did the job. I guess it's just you and me tonight" Lydia said to Tom as she wrapped her arms around Tom's neck. She started to rub the back of his neck.

"I guess it is darling. I truly missed you!"

"Me too honey" she answered, this time caressing his hair.

Unexpectedly, Lydia sank her head on Tom's chest and started crying.

"You want to talk about it honey?" Tom asked

"She is not going to make it Tom. She is so weak, and sick. I barely recognized my own sister!"

Tom rubbed her back and pulled her closer to him.

"I am so sorry sweetie. I wish I could do something for her. From now on, it will be god's will"

"It was not only the visit to the hospital. It was as if…" Lydia started "Lily and Charlie had this…special connection when they saw each other"

"What do you mean by special connection honey?" Tom asked Lydia

"Well, Lily had all of these tubes connected to her. She also had this oxygen mask strapped to her face to help her breathe, she looked so weak! Obviously she could not talk to us, but then…" Lydia hesitated to continue. She slowly pulled away from Tom's arms, sat on one of the dinner table chairs, and stared at Tom for almost a minute.

"What Lydia? What happened inside that room?" asked Tom

"Although she was unable to talk to us" she began to say shaking her head on disbelief, "I heard her voice Tom. I believe she was telling me how much she loved us. It was as if she wanted me to hear her last words. It was very odd Tom."

"Maybe she was able to take her mask for a few seconds, and you didn't notice Lydia"

"No she did not Tom. I am sure of it. I kept an eye on her the whole time we were inside her room" she quickly replied back

"I think you need a glass of this excellent wine to help you relax, honey."

"Tom, I am serious! Then, this old lady by the name of Claudia. She was so friendly with Charlie. She said something to him just before we went inside Lily's room to see her."

"Oh, I see. The same Claudia Charlie mentioned before" he said as he started pouring a glass of the wine for Lydia. "Here honey. I think you are under a lot of stress and you need to relax, ok?" Tom said sitting across her and pushing the glass of wine towards her.

In one gulp she drank half of the wine, and right away Tom refilled it.

"Are you trying to take advantage of me?" Lydia asked him

"Maybe hon. Just drink. It will make you feel better, I swear." Tom answered back with a slight grin on his face.

"Sorry dear." Lydia scratched her head. "Thanks for the great dinner you cooked for us, but I do not feel hungry at this moment" she said as she sipped more of the wine.

"We can eat it tomorrow honey, no problem." Tom replied

Lydia reached across the dinner table and grabbed both of Tom's hands. She had to remind herself of the great husband he was to her and of the great father he was to Charlie.

"Tom, sometimes I feel that I am going crazy"

"You are not Lydia. I assure you, you are not!"

"Why all of these strange things happening to me Tom?"

"I…don't know honey. You need to rest, I know that"

"I rested enough Tom. I want answers as to why these strange occurrences are happening to me. First, in Charlie's room, then at the market, and now while visiting Lily at the hospital. Don't you think it is strange? And in all circumstances, Charlie was with me."

"Lydia, you take Charlie almost everywhere you go."

"Yes, I know. But during all those instances, something felt different, unusual. I felt this…special connection with our son, Tom. A link I have never felt before" Lydia said

She then looked straight at Tom and said "Tom, I want Charlie to see a psychologist"

"A psychologist. You mean a shrink?" Tom asked taken by surprise

"No, not a shrink, Tom. I meant a licensed, experienced, psychologist that can maybe, explain what is going on"

"Lydia, honey, I don't think that would be a good idea"

"Why not? He had seen some before"

"Then why now? Why more shrink visits? You know he always hated going to those sessions"

"I want him to see a special psychologist this time. One that specializes in unusual…unexplainable… situations"

"You mean supernatural stuff…like ghosts, crap like that?"

"I need answers Tom!" Lydia exclaimed

"And you think Charlie seeing a person specializing in paranormal situations is the answer Lydia?"

Lydia grabbed Tom's hands tighter. "Yes I do Tom. I did some research and found this psychologist that has great credentials and is highly recommended that specializes on these type of cases"

"What is his name?"

"It's a woman. Her name is Abigail Lobowski. She got her PhD from Stanford University and she has been practicing on these cases for over twenty years."

Tom pulled his hands away and started shaking his head side to side as in doubt.

"As I said before Lydia, I do not think this is a good idea" said Tom

"Tell me why not? What do we have to lose?" Lydia replied

"Our sanity, our son?" said Tom

"Our son? Why would you say that Tom?" Lydia responded with anger "I want what is best for our son, Tom! I want Charlie to be…"

Tom abruptly stood up from the dinner table and interrupted Lydia "Normal? Charlie is not crazy Lydia. He is autistic. And the sooner you realize that the better is going to be for this family" he said furiously.

"Tom! I didn't mean it that way! I want what is best for Charlie. Something is happening here and you cannot see it. Oh my god!" Lydia then started crying uncontrollably.

Tom was still standing, hands firmly on his waist. They did not argue that often, and after this exchange he felt really bad, especially after seeing Lydia's reaction. He slowly sat back on the dinner table chair.

"I am sorry honey. I shouldn't have said that. It was stupid of me"

"Yes, it was very stupid Tom!" she cried back still covering her face.

Tom slowly grabbed her hands and pulled them down from her face.

"Sorry babe. I didn't mean it. I am frustrated just as you are. I want answers too. Please forgive me. Let's not argue anymore, ok?" said Tom

"Ok" replied Lydia while weeping and wiping away some of her tears.

Tom quickly grabbed a box of tissues from the breakfast bar and offered it to Lydia.

"If you think seeing this psychologist will be good for Charlie, then for god's sake, take him"

"I want *us* to take him Tom. Not just me. We must do this as a family" said Lydia to Tom

Tom gave a long sigh and then said "ok honey. We will both go"

Tom wiped away her tears with his left hand. He had to remind himself of the great wife she was to him and of the great mother she was to Charlie. He gave her a soft kiss on her lips.

"Can I take advantage of you now?" Tom asked. They both had a quick chuckle. Lydia pulled him closer and then whispered in his right ear. "Please, *do* take advantage of me tonight my love"

5

The Revelation

Doctor Lobowski's office was located at the Eastwood Medical Plaza, about six miles from Tom and Lydia's house. They had both agreed on a ten o'clock morning appointment and they were running a few minutes late. Tom drove the van and after going around the parking area three times he finally found an available space. The building was painted a light grey color with silver pop ups, with marble accents combining the specs of the grey and silver colors at the bottom. As they approached the building entrance Tom was already thinking about the cost of these expensive consultations, and worse, if they would be worth their time and money. But Lydia wanted seriously to give this a try and he was in no mood for another argument between them. As they were entering the elevator to reach the fourth floor Lydia could see the reservation on Tom's face. She could comprehend him very well now, after many years of marriage. But she did not say anything just as Tom kept his thoughts to himself. They arrived to suite number 410. Lydia let Charlie in first and right away they were greeted by an oriental looking receptionist with a name tag that said *Mae*. Mae asked for their last name.

"Winston. We have a ten o'clock appointment" said Lydia

"Please have a seat Mr. and Mrs. Winston. Doctor Lobowski will be with you all in a few minutes" Mae said cheerfully.

"Thank you" Lydia replied

Charlie sat down quietly looking around the office, collecting every bit of information about the new place they had just arrived at. The office was decorated with oriental vases, flowers, figurines, and delicate oriental artwork. The relaxing sound of cascading water spread throughout the room from a small fountain that had been placed strategically on one corner of the reception room. The flooring was a smooth dark wood, and on the center of it was a beautiful square picture of a purple orchid made out of marble.

"Mr. and Mrs. Winston, doctor Lobowski is ready to see you" Mae told them.

They entered doctor Lobowski's office who was standing ready to greet them.

"Hello Mrs. Winston, Mr. Winston. And this young man must be Charlie, correct?" she said shaking Charlie's hand last.

"Nice to meet you doctor Lobowski" Lydia said

"Nice to meet you too doc" Tom said

"Well, please sit down" doctor Lobowski said

Her office was as exquisitely decorated just as the reception area, in an oriental theme, with the exact copy of a picture of the purple orchid hanging on the left wall of her office. They were bookcases all around, and three stacks of folders were on her desk. Directly displayed behind her were numerous awards, letters of recognitions, photos with dignitaries, and two frames showing her degrees from Stanford University and MIT. Sometimes she spoke in fragments, to make sure that his patients clearly understood what she had told them.

"Mr. Winston…Mrs. Winston… how can I be of help to you?" she asked

"As we discussed on the phone doctor Lobowski" started Lydia, "I am very concerned with these unusual situations that have happened to me lately"

"Well… Mr. and Mrs. Winston… I've been reading and reviewing the initial consultation papers you sent me concerning Charlie's condition combined with your unusual experiences…and I'll have to say the least…your case sounds very interesting" the doctor said while viewing one of her folders.

Doctor Lobowski continued on "Mrs. Winston, let me ask you this. Is it something that your husband…Mr. Winston… has also experienced?"

"No. I am the only one that have experienced them, as far as I know"

Tom shook his head confirming Lydia's answer as soon as doctor Lobowski asked the question.

And Mrs. Winston… can you describe to me…in detail…exactly what has happened on those instances?"

"Well," Lydia cleared her throat twice and continued explaining to doctor Lobowski. "It has happened exactly three times now. During these instances, I felt as if my body was somewhere else, as if in a trance of some kind. And I think…I think I may have said something, but I feel as if isn't me who is talking. It's a very weird feeling," Lydia finished explaining while crossing her arms in front of her chest.

Doctor Lobowski was attentively listening to Lydia, both her hands on top of her desk, right one on top of the left one. She was only five feet two inches tall but her big office chair made her look taller as she lifted the chair all of the ways up almost until her small legs were dangling from the edge of the seat cushion. She wore thick glasses with big black frames because of some hereditary vision problem, her hair kind of messy, cheaply recently colored black hair, and in her late sixties. Tom thought to himself that she should have retired a long time ago, and that she looked as if she had just gotten out of bed, forgetting to brush her hair or teeth. He also thought she had an annoying voice, to top it all.

"Who else has been with you Mrs. Winston when these occurrences have happened to you?"

"Only Charlie" Lydia replied

"And…where exactly was Charlie…at the moment?" doctor Lobowski asked her

"Well, I always keep him close to me, just because of...his condition"

"You mean his autism...Mrs. Winston" the doctor replied

"Yes, his autism" said Lydia glancing at Tom. "One time, two years ago we decided to visit this new store during Christmas season, and he gave us a big scare. When we looked around he had disappeared, he was nowhere to be found. After about ten minutes that felt like a lifetime, we finally found him on the toy section of the store safe and sound"

Upon hearing this story, Charlie, who was quietly sitting staring at the ceiling brought his head down and gave doctor Lobowski the cynical smirk that Lydia hated so much. The doctor stared at him for a few seconds then gave Charlie a slight smile.

"So, during all of these experiences...Charlie has been...in close contact with you...and by that... I mean...within touching distance" said the doctor

"Of course" Lydia replied

After this last sentence doctor Lobowski noticed that Tom was fiddling with his cell phone and obviously was getting bored with their consultation. She wanted to draw him in so she turned to Tom.

"Mr. Winston, you can contribute... to our conversation anytime you feel like it. That is why all of you... are here, to share your experiences"

"No, no. It's ok. I am here just to observe doc, that's all"

"Tom! This is a family consultation, not just about me and Charlie" Lydia interrupted

Doctor Lobowski then injected "No, I understand your frustration and doubt... Mr. Winston. But tell me, what do you think is happening to your wife Lydia?"

"I really don't know doc. Like I told my wife many times before I think it is just stress. But you are the expert doc" Tom answered her.

Lydia gave Tom a stare while raising her eyebrows.

"Mr. Winston..." doctor Lobowski started to say "I may be the expert here...but we must...try to solve this problem together...you cannot alienate yourself from it. Do you understand?"

"Sorry doc. It's just that I am very reluctant about all of this" Tom said gesturing with his hands.

"About all of what, Mr. Winston?"

"This nonsense about unusual…paranormal…out of this world stuff"

"And by that you mean… the unexplained episodes experienced by your wife Lydia"

"Yes, that's what I mean. And of course Charlie has seen other psychologists before, and…I don't understand what my son Charlie has to do with these so called occurrences my wife is experiencing"

"But maybe is not only Charlie and Lydia that need my help, you may need it too"

"No, not me. I don't think I need any psychologists help, doc" said Tom

"Well, we will see about that Mr. Winston" doctor Lobowski replied

Doctor Lobowski turned to Lydia and asked her "Mrs. Winston, have you heard the term telepathy or thought transference?"

"Telepathy? Yes, I have heard of it" said Lydia

"Mr. and Mrs. Winston… the definition of telepathy itself covers a few categories. Like…mind reading…the ability to communicate with others…using only our thoughts…and even the ability to control other person's minds…or even their bodies"

"Hold on, doctor. Are you telling me that what it's been happening to me has something to do with telepathy?" Lydia asked stunned.

"No, not in that broad definition…as I stated…but I think in your situation we are dealing with some type of mind reading capacity. That is…the unique ability of being able to read… other person's thoughts"

Lydia was clearly astonished while Tom ran his fingers thru his hair and started to scratch his head.

After a short pause Lydia asked "So, what you are saying is that I have been reading other people's minds, without me knowing it?"

"No, not you Mrs. Winston. But I believe Charlie has" she replied while glancing at Charlie.

Tom suddenly sprung from the office couch "That's it! This is a lot of BS! Let's go back home Lydia!"

"Tom, please sit down and let's hear what the doctor has to say!" Lydia yelled back

"You expect me to believe that our son has something to do with all of this horseshit of an explanation?"

"Tom, don't!" Lydia pleaded

Unexpectedly, doctor Lobowski stood up from her chair, put the tip of her fingers on top of her desk, and like a mama bear protecting her cub yelled back at Tom "Sit down Mr. Winston!"

She really looked much taller now and Tom quickly did as instructed. Doctor Lobowski then looked directly at Tom and spoke to him with an irate tone "Mr. Winston, let me tell you…that there has been…numerous research papers…articles…documentaries…clinical research…and documented cases…associating telepathy powers with autistic children. You can do the research yourself…at the library…or…as they call it today, google it…to learn more about his phenomena. Some have been autistic children, others Savant children. So, the fact is…Mr. Winston, is that Charlie clearly manifests some type of… mind reading aptitude, and whether you like it or not… you and your wife must learn how to live with it. Now… if you do not want my help… my office door is open, and you all can leave anytime you want."

Tom and Lydia stared at each other for a few seconds, Lydia clearly giving the sign of her desire to stay and find more about this extraordinary circumstances. "Please, honey" Lydia said to Tom.

Tom agreed with her by nodding his head but obviously with skepticism on his face.

Mama bear Lobowski sat down back on her tall office chair while keeping eye contact with Tom.

"Well, I am glad that this is all clear" she said to both Tom and Lydia

"I am so confused, doctor Lobowski. How does our son Charlie relates to all of this?" asked Lydia

"Mr. and Mrs. Winston, let me explain it the best way I can"

Doctor Lobowski took a large writing pad out of his top right hand desk drawer and started to draw some pictures. After a few seconds she then turned the pad around to show Tom and Lydia what she had drawn. To the best of Tom's knowledge they looked like two pictures of two antennas.

"Pardon me Mrs. Winston but I am an awful artist. Let me explain…on the simplest terms…what I think is happening in your case. Just like any radio communications… there is always two antennas… the one here on the right side… is the transmitting antenna. The one I drew here on the left side… is the receiver antenna." She then took her pen and wrote *Charlie* under the picture of the transmitting antenna, and *Lydia* under the picture of the receiving antenna.

Doctor Lobowski then continued with her explanation to Tom and Lydia "This is what I believe is happening Mrs. Winston. Charlie… is using his unique gift of mind reading… and transmitting these people's thoughts to you. In other words, Mrs. Winston… you are his receiver. You are essentially the receiver of his thoughts."

"Someone else's thoughts? What about his own?" asked Lydia

"I believe he can, but he can be very selective, allowing you only to receive what he wants you to receive"

Lydia got up from the couch and started pacing nervously around doctor Lobowski's office.

"Why me, why now?" she asked

"Lydia, may I call you Lydia?" asked doctor Lobowski

"Yes, by all means"

"As you both know by now autistic children are very withdrawn… reserved, always into their own world. I strongly believe… this is a way for Charlie… to communicate with you, to be closer to you."

"Have you seen cases like this before?"

"I have seen many cases in my many years of practice…that resemble what you are experiencing…but if we can prove and collaborate what you are telling me here today…then…Charlie would be the only case I have ever encountered…of full mind reading and transmitting ability"

"And how does this exactly happen? All of a sudden, he decides to read some stranger's mind?"

"I think the process starts by way of touch. You see… when Charlie decides to read someone and you happen to touch him…he starts basically transmitting whatever that person is thinking to you, the receiver. Hence…I am sure…that is when you experience…these trance like episodes. But you must learn…how to control this special gift that you now have with your son."

"What do you mean?" asked Lydia

"You told me earlier during our consultation…that when these occurrences happen you feel as if words come out of your mouth… but you believe they are not your words" doctor Lobowski said.

"Yes I did. It feels like that. Very awkward"

"Well…what you have to control Lydia…is the ability…to keep those messages you are receiving from Charlie to yourself…without having to scream them out loud…and embarrassing other people and yourself. Remember…these messages that you are receiving… are actually other people's thoughts…and you are screaming them out to the world. Do you understand?" the doctor explained.

"And how she is supposed to do that doc?" Tom asked suddenly

"Well…like anything else Mr. Winston, it takes practice and patience. She must really concentrate on the messages Charlie is sending her, she must not be scared, or nervous, of what is happening to her. She must understand…that what she is experiencing…is a very special, unique gift…a special type of bond with her son. She must realize that these occurrences are nothing to be scared about…but just the opposite…to see it as a way to communicate and get closer to her autistic son"

"Can we try it now?" asked Lydia

"Try what honey?" Tom asked her

"The readings with Charlie"

"It is up to you Lydia, if you are up to it" doctor Lobowski said

"No! No way. You are not getting our son thru that situation again." Tom yelled back

"Lydia, we can really use the help of your doubtful husband here" the doctor said pointing to Tom

"Please do this for me honey, I am begging you" Lydia said to Tom

Tom continued shaking his head, unwilling to participate on the experiment.

"Mrs. Winston, will you give me your consent to videotape the session if you decide to do it?"

"Sure, no problem doctor" Lydia answered

Tom grabbed Lydia's left hand tight, slightly shaking and asked her "Honey, what if something happens to Charlie? We will never forgive ourselves"

"Mr. Winston…" doctor Lobowski started "it is not Charlie the one I am worried about. I am more worried about you and your reaction afterwards"

Tom was still clenching Lydia's hand and said; "if it is for our son well being, I will do whatever is necessary. I am ready"

Doctor Lobowski had positioned a small video camera on a tripod pointing directly at the three of them. She stood behind it, and only her voice could be heard.

"The video camera is ready, and we are ready to record the session" the doctor said.

Doctor Lobowski asked Lydia "Mrs. Winston, may I have a few words with Charlie?"

"Sure doctor"

The doctor slowly approached Charlie who was now staring at the ceiling. She sat in front of him.

"Charlie, can you look at me for a few minutes please?"

"Yes" Charlie quickly replied.

"Charlie, your mom and dad are going to try a simple experiment. We want you to be part of it. Just as you do in school. Ok? Are you ok with this Charlie?"

Charlie then stared at the doctor for a few seconds before answering her.

"I guess…what kind of experiment?"

"Charlie, what I want you to do… is to look straight at your dad… while sitting here, and *listen* carefully to what he has to say to you. Can you do that for me?" doctor Lobowski asked

"I guess…" Charlie replied

"But you really need to concentrate and really *listen* to your dad. Ok?"

Charlie nodded his head in agreement.

"Now…" the doctor continued while looking at Charlie "your mom is going to stand right behind you with her hands on your shoulders, like this" she said as she motioned to Lydia to approach him. She stood up and rested both hands on Charlie's shoulders.

Doctor Lobowski wanted to assure Charlie that everything was going to be fine and that his parents were in no danger.

"Are you ready Charlie? Remember, I want you to really *listen* to everything your dad says to you" doctor Lobowski repeated to Charlie while emphasizing the word *listen*.

"Ok" replied Charlie

Doctor Lobowski then turned to Tom and said softly to him "Mr. Winston, I want you to relax… and just think about anything that comes to your mind. You do not have to look at Charlie. Just pretend you are at home… relaxing after a long day at work…understand?"

"Yes doc. I get it. Just sit here and do nothing but think, right?"

"You got it Tom" Lobowski answered. "Ready Charlie?" She asked him while moving behind the camera. She then pressed the record button.

"Today is May 3rd, 2018. It is eleven AM and we are inside my office. Mr. and Mrs. Winston have given me permission… along with their son Charlie Winston… to record this session regarding a possible case… of thought transference ability with her son Charlie. There have been three other probable manifestations… as explained by Mrs. Winston and we want to establish… the relationship of her son's telepathic powers and the possibility of her as the receiver."

Charlie stared at his dad, then, within seconds, that unique smirk came to his face while Lydia stood up right behind him, hands firmly on his shoulders, her eyes closed.

"Relax, Tom. Relax, Lydia" doctor Lobowski assured them.

Two minutes passed then three, then five. Then, unannounced, Lydia's body felt limp, her eyes heavy, and right away she felt that weird trance like feeling within her.

Tom started to get up from the couch as if trying to catch her before she would fall to the floor. But doctor Lobowski intervened. Doctor Lobowski immediately signaled at him to sit still.

"Mr. Winston, no!" she whispered to Tom

Tom then heard Lydia's voice while her eyes were still closed. *"What is wrong with my wife?"* Lydia started saying *"Oh my god! It looks like she is going to faint! I knew this shrink visit was a bad idea. This is just bullshit, a waste of time. Shit, I rather be home drinking a beer and watching the ladies UFC bouts. And this old lady, my god! She should be at home kneading a sweater or playing bingo instead of pushing all of this mumbo jumbo to Lydia. I love you honey, you and Charlie are my everything, but I do not believe on this telepathy crap. What? What are you saying? Are you repeating what I am saying…I mean…thinking? What is going on? Charlie, quit looking at me like that! Charlie, Lydia, enough!"* Tom suddenly jumped from the couch and grabbed Lydia as she released her hands from Charlie's shoulders and wobbled from side to side as if she had just awakened from a long dream. After helping Lydia to the couch he walked and stood by doctor's Lobowski's office door. Tom looked pale, confused, dumbfounded. Lydia suddenly opened her eyes.

"Tom, are you alright?" Lydia asked

"Are you?" Tom asked back standing by the door. "No…no I am not…hell no I am not! I am not…alright. What in the hell happened here doc?" asked Tom angrily.

"Mr. Winston, please be calm. You have just experienced… the first reading from your son thru your wife Lydia" doctor Lobowski tried to explain.

"No, no. That is impossible! I did not say anything to my son! My lips did not move! I was just there…just…just…thinking…how can this be doc? This is not natural, it is not possible!" Tom asked still astonished.

"Well…Tom, we just proved it is indeed possible. Do you want to see? I recorded it all, here on my camera. Or, maybe you want to try it again, Mr. Winston" she added.

"No, hell I am not! Neither is my wife or my son, doc!" Tom yelled back

"I understand Mr. Winston…just wanted to prove my point. I think we have strong confirmation now… of Charlie's incredible telepathic *and* transmitting capabilities" doctor Lobowski reaffirmed him

"Honey, are you ok? How are you?" Lydia asked as she got closer to Tom. Tom started shaking his head incredulous as to what had just occurred inside the doctor's office.

Lydia then asked doctor Lobowski "Doctor, did I said anything? My mind is not clear if I did"

"You did Lydia, you sure did" Tom said to her

"Like what, exactly. What did I say?"

"Well…" Tom started saying; but the doctor abruptly cut in and turned to Lydia.

"You said a few words about how much Tom loves you and your son…and something about not trusting me… oh, by the way, Mr. Winston, I hate Bingo. I think it is a stupid and boring game"

"What? Bingo? Where did that come from?" asked Lydia

"Nothing, Lydia" said the doctor. "Your husband thinks I should be home playing little grandma, that's all…"

"Sorry doc. I didn't mean any insult" Tom replied

"None taken Mr. Winston"

"You can call me Tom, doc"

"None taken, Tom. Like I told you before, I clearly understand your doubts… about all of this. But now I hope you can… look at this in a different perspective. I hope…this has changed your mind… somewhat"

"Yes it has doc. Thanks for your help and understanding"

"Can we see the recording doctor?" asked Lydia

"I have to…study it…take some notes…perhaps during our next session. I think we had enough for today, don't you think? You and your family need to rest." Doctor Lobowski answered

"Yes honey. Doctor Lobowski is right. We should be heading home" agreed Tom

"Ok. I guess we should be going then. Thanks for your help doctor. Please let us know when we can view the recording" said Lydia

"I sure will Lydia"

"Charlie, honey…are you ready to go home?" Lydia asked him

Charlie answered while staring at the floor. "Yes mom. Let's go home. Yes, let's go home mom"

Charlie stood up, took a few short steps towards the door, head still staring down at the floor. He stood next to Tom who gave him a hug and a kiss on the forehead. "How you doing, buddy?" Tom asked Charlie. Charlie did not respond.

"Goodbye Charlie. And thank you for your cooperation. You were great Charlie. Hope to see you again. Agreed?" Doctor Lobowski offered to shake his hand but Charlie did not comply.

"Let's go home mom. Let's go home. I want to go home" Charlie kept repeating

Doctor Lobowski extended her hand to Tom and Lydia and they shook hands.

"Thanks for coming Mr. and Mrs. Winston. It was a pleasure to meet you all. I will be talking to you soon. Oh… and here is my card. If you have any questions or concerns please feel free to call me. My personal mobile number is there" she said while handing out her business card to Tom.

"What now, doctor?" Tom asked opening the door slightly.

"Nothing, Tom" she then turned to Lydia. "Lydia has now a very good idea of what is happening to her and hopefully… will learn how to control this unique gift. Again…practice and patience. Practice and patience. The more she has control over this the more it will come to her naturally. She must have control over this power, and not the other way around…understand?"

"Yes doctor, we understand. Thank you so much for your help" Lydia told her while embracing doctor Lobowski and giving her a hug.

"You are very welcome. Will be seeing you again soon"

"Thank you doctor" Tom said as he opened the office door and all three exited.

Doctor Lobowski stood in front of her opened office door long after Lydia, Tom and Charlie had left. She then turned around and looked at her small video camera. Mae, her receptionist, came back in.

"Doctor Lobowski, doctor Lobowski? Are you ready for your next patient?" Mae asked her; but the doctor did not answer. "Doctor Lobowski, are you well? Are you ok?" she added in her strong Korean accent.

"Oh my God! This is just incredible! I finally found one!" she whispered to herself.

On their way home Tom and Lydia did not say much to each other. Lydia rested her head against the passenger door window. Charlie sat as usual, quiet on the backseat staring outside. Tom took a glance at him thru the rearview mirror.

"Are you ok Charlie?" he asked him

"Yes, I am ok" Charlie responded

"How about you Tom? Are you ok? You kind of freaked out inside the doctor's office" Lydia said. Her head was still resting on the window while talking to Tom.

"I am fine honey. It's not every day that you get to experience anything like that, especially with your family" Tom replied.

"Do you think I am a freak?"

"No I don't honey. Why would you ask that" Tom said rubbing her leg.

"Are you jealous…that I have this special connection with Charlie now and you don't?"

"Why would I be Lydia? This is something you always longed for. And anyways…" Tom shrugged his shoulders "I know that there is always a strong connection between sons and their mothers"

"Are you sure honey?" Lydia asked now looking at Tom.

"Yes. I am sure. I love you babe"

"Love you too. And thanks for being so understanding during our visit with doctor Lobowski. I know you still have your doubts"

"No problem Lydia. I want to do what is best for our family honey"

"I know you do Tom. I know you do" Lydia added squeezing his hand.

After this, nothing else was said inside the van concerning their visit to Dr. Lobowski's office. When they pulled into their driveway they were surprised to see their sixteen year old neighbor Mayra already walking towards them. Lydia thought that she must have been checking every five minutes for their arrival. Lydia got out of the van and Mayra approached her from the passenger's side.

"Hello Mrs. Winston" Mayra said with her sweet smile.

"Hi Mayra. Nice to see you" Lydia replied.

Tom got out and started to unbuckle Charlie from the back seat. Mayra waved to him from the passenger side and gave him her soft, cute, and girly smile.

"Hello Mr. Winston"

"Oh…hello Mayra. How are you doing?"

"Fine, I am doing just fine. How are you?"

"Trying to survive. How are your parents?"

"They are doing well. They say hello"

Lydia cut into their chat and asked Mayra "So, What brings you to our driveway Mayra. Need help with something?" she asked staring her down.

Mayra was wearing a tight black summer dress that contoured her body very well. Lydia thought to herself that it was too promiscuous and inappropriate for a sixteen year old girl. She noticed right away the low cleavage on the dress, showing half of her young, soft, and perky breasts and her nipples pointing right at her. She was kind of jealous of those young breasts and at the same time mad that Charlie was being *raped* again right in front of her eyes. Charlie rushed towards Mayra and quickly Lydia grabbed his arm trying to push him behind her. Tom came around from the driver's side.

"How can we help you Mayra?" he asked her

"Oh…nothing important Tom. I just wanted to invite you…I mean, invite you all to my seventeenth birthday celebration. My parents are throwing a party for me and thought you…I mean you and Mrs. Winston, and Charlie would like to come"

"Can we come mom? Can we come to Mayra's party mom?" Charlie asked excited

"Well Mayra, we will need to see if we have anything planned for the weekend. Plus my sister is still at the hospital. We will have to let you know later"

"I want to go mom! I want to go!" Charlie exclaimed

"We'll see honey…ok?"

"But I want to go mom! I want to go to Mayra's party" repeated Charlie

Lydia squeezed his arm hard "I told you already, we will see" she said, this time giving him a serious stare.

"Can you believe I am almost an adult? Almost eighteen?" Mayra said looking at Tom

"Yes. You almost are Mayra. You have grown into a very nice lady" Tom answered politely

"Thank you Tom"

Lydia turned to Tom who she noticed was also admiring Mayra's black dress.

"Tom, honey. Can you bring those bags from the car inside the house please?"

"Bags, what bags?" asked Tom

"*The bags*. The ones you need to bring inside…"

"Oh…sure honey. Right away. Nice to see you Mayra" Tom said

"Goodbye Tom. Hope you…I mean all of you can attend my party on Saturday" said Mayra. She then crossed her arms under her breasts and pushed them up while Tom walked away inside the house. Charlie thought she was the most beautiful thing he had ever seen. Charlie was still staring at Mayra when he felt his mother's hands on his shoulders.

"Practice and patience, practice and patience" she remembered doctor Lobowski's words.

Within five seconds of her touching Charlie she felt the heaviness on her eyes, her eyes wanting to close, and that trance like feeling again.

"You must learn how to control the power, and not the other way around" she remembered doctor Lobowski telling her.

This time she kept her eyes open and her mouth closed. She could see Mayra. She could *hear* Mayra. But her lips were not moving. She could *hear* her voice but her mouth was closed. Mayra was not talking to her. But she clearly could hear Mayra's voice, coming from somewhere. She unmistakably heard her say; *"Sorry Charlie but your dad is a darn hottie. I hope he comes to my birthday party Saturday. He makes me so hot! He would take off my red panties, and I would wrap them around his neck! Then he would lick my body slowly…"* Lydia suddenly took her hands off Charlie's shoulders.

"You little bitch" Lydia whispered to herself.

Mayra gave Lydia a peculiar look and asked her "What did you say Mrs. Winston? Are you ok?"

"No, nothing. Just talking to myself" Lydia answered

"Well. I hope you all can come to my house Saturday then." Mayra responded with her soft smile.

"We will try our best. Goodbye Mayra"

"That little tramp, she really wants to seduce my husband!" Lydia thought

At this moment Lydia had just realized that she had control over the readings. She remembered, she understood the conveyance of thoughts from her son to her, as his receiver. Mayra was turning away towards her parents home when Lydia suddenly called her back. "Mayra?" she said to her.

She motioned Charlie to stay where he was and got very close to Mayra. She then whispered into her ear. "Just wanted to tell you Mayra, my husband does not like red colored panties. He likes them black." Mayra's eyes opened wide as if she had seen a ghost and started to walk backwards towards her house without taking her eyes off Lydia.

Lydia couldn't help herself "Oh... and Mayra?" Mayra stopped abruptly. Her eyes were still wide open, and she then swallowed hard.

"And that thing about wrapping them around his neck, too kinky!" Lydia said to her with a grin.

Mayra turned around, scratched her left arm with some bushes, almost fell, and ran inside her house as if an ugly witch was about to swallow her whole. Lydia grabbed Charlie by his right arm and pulled him towards their front door.

"Come on honey" she said "she is not your type."

Lydia walked into the kitchen where Tom was searching inside the pantry for something to eat. Charlie went upstairs straight to his room and started playing his Michael Jackson *Thriller* album.

"Hey, honey. You talked for a while with Mayra. Were you talking about the party?" he said

"I swear, that girl has the hots for you. She practically threw herself at you today. And that dress, oh my god! She wanted to make sure you saw all of her tits!" Lydia said furiously.

"Come on, Lydia. Lots of teenagers have crushes on many people. They have crushes on their teachers, friends, and famous persons. That is very common."

"Yea. But she has a real crush on you Tom. And poor Charlie. He is fixated with her. And calling you Tom? What happened to Mr. Winston? That little slut, I swear..."

"Don't say that honey. She is a good kid. She is just going thru puberty, that's all." Tom tried to assure her.

"I just have a feeling, she is a no good little nymphomaniac" Lydia replied

"And…what makes you say that?"

"I just have this little hunch…"

"Did you tell her we were going to her party?"

"No. I just told her I would think about it." Lydia looked back towards their front door. "Anyhow, it is not me or Charlie she is interested on seeing there Saturday" she said

6

Carondelet Palace, Quito, Ecuador

President Melancón was admiring the beautiful gardens and surroundings of Carondelet Palace from his Presidential office window apartment located on the third floor. At the age of forty one he was now the youngest ever elected leader of Ecuador. He was now ready to bring serious changes to his beloved country, eradicate poverty, and fight the big foreign corporations that have been draining his country's resources. He saw in Hugo Chavez, the former Venezuelan leader, as a mentor for his socialist plans. And with Russian president Perchenko he saw a strategic ally to spread his ideals to all of central and South America. He preferred to be called *'Señor Presidente'* [Mr. President] instead of *'Mi Presidente'* [My President], as some of his fellow citizens used to call him. His office door opened and his chief of staff rushed in.

"Mr. President. The honorable Russian President Perchenko has arrived" he said.

"Very well, let him in Manuel" Melancón replied.

Russian President Nikolai Perchenko entered the office followed by a group of seven other men. His personal translator was to his right.

"Welcome, welcome to the people of Ecuador's Presidential residence, President Perchenko" Melancón greeted him extending his right hand to Perchenko. He then motioned him to sit on a wine colored leather chair. Melancón sat in front of him except that his chair was slightly taller. Melancón turned to his own personal translator and asked him "Ask the President if he would like a Cuban cigar"

"No thank you. I do not smoke Mr. President" Perchenko said thru his translator.

"Do you mind if I have one?" he asked while picking one from a fancy carved wooden box.

"No I do not mind. After all, this is your house".

"Well, that is true, isn't it? These are the best cigars in the world. Imported from Cuba. But this special brand cost almost ten thousand dollars per case. This one was sent to me by Raul Castro on the day of my inauguration".

"Enjoy it Mr. President" Perchenko said.

While the Ecuadorian President lit up his Cuban cigar Perchenko started whispering something to his translator. His translator then gestured to one of the men behind them. One of them then handled him a thin manila colored envelope.

"Mr. President, here are the details of the transaction as you instructed"

Perchenko carefully placed the envelope on the middle of the table between them.

"Right down to business, Mr. Perchenko? No cigar, no girls, no pleasures? May I offer you and your men something to eat from our great Ecuadorian cuisine?"

"I am sorry Mr. President but I am on a very busy schedule. I must return to The Kremlin by this afternoon. But thank you for your generous offer" Perchenko answered.

Melancón inhaled from his cigar and let out a big draft of smoke into the room. He stared at Perchenko for a few seconds. He then turned to Manuel, his chief of staff.

"Manuel, can you check it please?" he asked him in a low tone of voice.

Manuel opened the manila envelope and started reading the contents silently.

"As you instructed Mr. President" Perchenko started "we have deposited one hundred fifty million dollars into a Swiss account. The deposit confirmation and access code are included in that page. You are welcome to confirm it, if you wish..."

Melancón glanced at Manuel, who upon finishing reading the document gave him a confirmation sign by nodding his head.

"No. No need President Perchenko. All is well. On behalf of the people of Ecuador I thank you for your generous contribution to our country".

"We are in agreement then, that my Russian ships will have access to the Galapagos Archipelago, navigation of our ships on Ecuadorian territorial waters and full assistance from your Navy as well."

"Yes, of course Mr. Perchenko. But you know, the United States government is already sniffing around. Wondering...about our alliance."

"Let me worry about the Americans Mr. President. In the meantime you just enjoy your Cuban cigars and this new beautiful home" said Perchenko gesturing with his hands and looking around Melancón's office.

"Are you sure you do not want to try one of these excellent cigars?"

"No. I am sure. As I stated before I do not smoke. Plus, I consider it one of the nastiest habits a person can have" Perchenko answered with a serious look on his face.

"Sorry you feel that way President Perchenko. By the way, Mr. Perchenko" Melancón said leaning forward, "Do you know the difference between enjoying a good cigar and a beautiful woman?"

"No I do not Mr. President."

"Well... a good cigar never talks back to you. You just...enjoy it. Nice, and quiet." Melancón responded as he inhaled again and let out another puff from his mouth. He then let out a loud laugh while his front teeth grinded on the cigar.

"Well, I'll have to agree with you on that Mr. President" said Perchenko with a light smile.

The two men couldn't be any more different. Perchenko was an avid sportsman and health nut while President Melancón enjoyed his Cuban cigars, loose women, and greasy foods. Perchenko had been married to his high school sweetheart for almost twenty five years while Melancón had been married twice and rumors of having at least three mistresses. The Russian President was a slender six feet and two inches tall. The Ecuadorian leader was five feet eight inches tall weighing almost two hundred fifty pounds. One was dressed in expensive Armani suits while the other wore khaki pants reminiscent of the Castro revolutionary era and cheap short sleeve shirts. One was clean shaven while the other one wore a frizzy, untrimmed beard, sideburns, and eyebrows. One President was motivated by absolute power while the other one was motivated by pure greed. But there was one thing that these two men had in common. It was the desire to bring geopolitical chaos to an already fragile world.

Perchenko did not really enjoyed Melancón's company but he needed him for now and tried to make the best of it without insulting the newly elected Ecuadorian President. He suddenly stood up and at the same time his entourage started to move around ready to leave.

"I do apologize Mr. President. But I must leave at this very moment. I have enjoyed your company as well as your joke, Mr. President." Perchenko said extending his hand to Melancón. As they shook hands Melancón responded "I am glad you have President Perchenko."

"We will be in touch again soon."

"Yes, yes, of course"

Four of the seven men walked out first in front of Perchenko while the other three walked behind him. They left Melancón's office and took Russian President Perchenko directly to the Ilyushin II Presidential plane. As soon as Perchenko left the Carondelet Palace grounds Melancón picked up and glanced at the single sheet of paper that contained the bank transfer confirmation. He called Manuel to his office.

"Manuel, check the deposit. Make sure that everything is in order."

Manuel took the paper and logged into a computer right away. A few minutes later Manuel came back.

"Everything is in order Mr. President. The one hundred fifty million dollars have been deposited to the account" he said to the Ecuadorian President.

"Thanks Manuel. This is all for now. Thanks for your help"

"Mi placer señor Presidente" Manuel replied in Spanish. He then left the Presidential office.

President Melancón sat back on his Presidential chair in front of his Presidential desk. He took a long puff from his expensive Cuban cigar and let out two rings of grey smoke from his mouth. A sarcastic grin came to his face.

'*Cabrones Rusos*' [Fucking Russians] he said to himself.

Two days after the meeting at Carondelet Palace President Perchenko woke up at exactly five in the morning. He was ready to start his six mile jog as he always did three times a week. His security detail closely followed him. An armored vehicle was in front of him with five men inside all carrying AK-47 weapons. Another one followed close behind with the same security arrangement. Two other husky Russian bodyguards ran alongside him, each wearing pistols on both hips, each loaded with twenty bullet clips. It was a crispy and cool morning below the Russian sky as Perchenko started his morning six mile run. Halfway thru his run the rear armored vehicle approached Perchenko on his left side. The man on the passenger side screamed at Perchenko while he was still running.

"President Perchenko, the waterways are fully open now" he yelled.

"Good. Tell Admiral Abramov to send in the first ships." he quickly replied.

He then immediately picked up the pace of his run while both of his bodyguards followed.

"Come on you bums!" he screamed at one of them "you better keep up, or I will shoot both of you myself!"

7

The day had finally come. Tom could not believe that he was sitting along with all of his colleagues at the FBI building graduation auditorium waiting anxiously to receive his badge and credentials after being sworn in. They were a few short speeches by the Vice President, the US Attorney General and the FBI director. Lydia had accompanied him but was waiting outside until the ceremony was complete. It did not sit well with Charlie when he had to sit for long periods of time anywhere, especially when he was away from home. They were both looking around the building when Lydia felt a tap on her left shoulder. Lydia turned around. It was Tom.

"How is Charlie doing honey" he asked

"Very well babe. No worries. He is just exploring around, as always. Let me see, let me see…!" she asked Tom

Tom reached inside his jacket pocket and pulled out his new black credential wallet with the gold embossed FBI badge. Before he handed it to Lydia to inspect he rubbed his right hand over the badge. He felt an enormous pride.

"Here. This is what I have worked so hard for" he said

After staring at it for about a minute Lydia did not say anything back at Tom. She suddenly gave Tom a long hug while tightly holding the black credential wallet on her right hand.

"I am so, so proud of you honey!" she exclaimed

"Thank you dear. And thanks for all of the support you have given me during this long process" Tom said back. He then gave her a kiss.

Tom looked around for Charlie and he saw that he was a few feet away pacing back and forth staring at the floor.

"Charlie, buddy, come here to dad" Tom asked him

Charlie quickly walked towards Tom and hugged him.

"How are you doing son?"

"Good" Charlie answered

"Charlie, do you want to see something real cool? Look" Tom said showing him his FBI credentials. "Isn't this awesome Charlie? Dad is officially an FBI Agent."

"Yea...FBI Agent. What is that dad?"

"It means that dad can put away bad people; so the good people in our country can feel safe buddy"

From the corner of his eye he saw Darren exiting the auditorium.

"Hey Darren!" said Tom said as he waved to him to come over. They shook hands and pat each other's backs.

"Congratulations! We made it Tom! Look at this. Isn't it great?" Darren said while looking at his new badge.

"I'm very proud of you both" Lydia injected

"Oh, I'm sorry Mrs. Winston. How are you? I was so thrilled that I did not see you there" Darren replied as he shook Lydia's hand.

"No. No need to apologize. You should be excited. This time belongs to the both of you"

"Yes. It sure does my friend" Tom agreed while shaking Darren's shoulder.

"Are you all ready to celebrate?" Darren asked

"Yes we are Darren. Come on Charlie"

"What are we celebrating dad? Dad, what are we celebrating?"

Tom kneeled in front of Charlie, and looking straight into his eyes he responded "the newly sworn in FBI Agent Thomas L. Winston my son."

Most of the new FBI agents did not get assigned to their preferred field office locations but Tom was able to stay in Fredericksburg because of Charlie's condition and the special school he attended. The next morning Tom was issued the Glock 23 forty caliber handgun from the vault. Just before he was about to open his car door to head home his cell phone rang. He immediately recognized the phone number as that of Mr. *Big D.*

"Good morning sir" Tom answered

"Good morning Agent Winston, and congratulations by the way" Domenico said on the other end.

"Thank you sir. Appreciate it. Could not have done it without your support and mentorship sir"

"You are welcome agent Winston. Listen, I know it's a last minute request but I need you and agent Johnson to stop by my office as soon as you can. There has been new developments regarding the Galapagos Islands situation and need to brief you both on it" Domenico said

"No problem sir"

"Ok. See you soon then" replied *Big D*

After ending his phone conversation with Domenico Tom dialed Lydia's number. "Hello honey. How you doing?" she answered the phone line.

"Great babe. Just picked up my weapon from the vault. I was about to head home but I just received a call from Mr. Domenico. He wants to see me as soon as possible. Can we meet for lunch tomorrow instead?"

"No problem hun. Go ahead. Me and Charlie will grab something and take it home."

"Sorry about the last minute change Lydia"

"It's ok Tom. Don't worry. You are a full time FBI agent now. I better get used to it, I understand"

"Thank you honey. Say hello to Charlie and give him a big hug from dad"

"I will Tom. Love you and proud of you. Goodbye honey"

"Love you both too. Goodbye" Tom responded

Tom arrived at Domenico's office later that morning. Upon arrival he noticed that Darren was already there. He was chatting with *Big D* and was wearing his dark suit required by all FBI agents. A light blue tie contrasted well with his dark jacket and he thought it made him look more elegant than he actually was. Tom knocked on the halfway opened door and Domenico waved him to come in. He then asked Darren.

"How in the hell you got here so quick? Do you happen to sleep on these hallways?"

"Yes Tom. I love it here!" Darren exclaimed with a light laugh

"Did they issue you gents your weapons?" asked *Big D*

"Yes sir." said Darren. He then slid the right side of his jacket towards his back to show his piece. "Pretty isn't she?"

"Good. Now the hard work starts gentlemen" Domenico assured them

He then picked up a manila folder from his desk. It had a red colored cover marked *SECRET/ SPECIAL ACCESS REQUIRED*. He handed it to Darren. Tom came closer and sat beside him.

"Gentlemen, as you will see on these files we have tentative intelligence that a meeting occurred between Perchenko and Melancón about two weeks ago at the Ecuadorian Carondelet Presidential residence. Satellite pictures confirmed that the Russian Presidential plane was indeed at the Quito International Airport"

"Any information from the ground sir?" Tom asked

"Not yet. We have been unable at this time to confirm the encounter between the two. We are trying our best to find reliable human intel to support this"

"Any idea how long the meeting was?" asked Darren

"No we don't agent Johnson. All we know is that Perchenko's plane left the same day around 2200 hours. But we cannot pinpoint the length of the meeting since like I said our intel on the ground is not reliable. But, as you can further read from this report we have also noticed unusual activity from the Russian Northern Fleet located here, in Severomorsk" Domenico said pointing at a map included on the report. "The Northern Fleet is commanded by a long time ally of Perchenko, Admiral Alexander Abramov"

Darren took a long breath then asked "Sir, do you think they are getting ready to sail to Ecuadorian waters?"

"I'm almost sure they are son. We cannot let this out to the media. It will be chaos out there. We do not want a repeat of the Cuban Missile Crisis on our hands. Understood?" Domenico emphasized.

"Understood sir" Darren answered

"Sir, can I ask you a question?" Tom asked reluctantly.

"Sure. Go ahead agent Winston"

"Well, sir, I have not heard or seen anything else regarding this situation, about Ecuador and the Russian Federation. Can I ask you how you obtained this report?"

Domenico took a few steps towards a curio cabinet that was at a corner of his office. A carefully folded American flag was displayed inside a pyramid shape case. It had been given to him by a fellow Vietnam soldier who had later died supposedly from complications of Agent Orange. While staring at it Domenico answered Tom. "I have a good friend who really cares agent Winston. A person who cares about the safety and future of our country, instead of the usual fucking politics and red tape."

Tom started scratching his head as it was apparent *Big D* was reluctant on discussing any more information about his source.

"Does this person works for the agency?"

"No. This person does not agent Winston. Any more questions? Do you want a name? Do you really want a name?"

"No sir. It's ok. I understand your situation" replied Tom

Domenico turned around and faced Tom.

"His name is Simon. Like Simon Cowell, the famous british tv celebrity. Just Simon...

"Got it sir" replied Tom

"But let's not talk about my source agent Winston. Instead, let's talk about what we can do as FBI Intelligence agents to find out what are these pricks up to. My intel, although good, has been very limited and we still do not know the specifics of that meeting at Carondelet. Like I told you earlier before you graduated; I consider both of you to be my best intelligence officers and I need both of you to apply all you have learned here and extract all the information you can from all of your contacts out there."

"How much time do we have sir?" asked Tom

"Don't know exactly. But the latest intel tells us that the Northern Fleet will be sailing any minute now. And we also do not know how many missiles or nuclear warheads they are carrying."

"Sir, do you expect another meeting between Perchenko and Melancón soon?" asked Darren

"Yes I do agent Johnson. And if they have one we expect it to be in Quito again." Domenico answered

"Why Quito again sir? Why not the Kremlin?"

"For what I have heard about him Melancón is pissy about flying. He is a very superstitious man. Plus, he is very reluctant about leaving his Presidential residence. He is always worried that someone might try to assassinate him and/or his family. He is always surrounded only by a very special security detail hand picked by him and two to three political advisors. Look gentlemen, all we need is a break on good and reliable intel to find out what these two are planning next ok?"

What about Deputy Secretary Mallory sir?" Tom asked him

"What about him agent Winston?"

"Do you want us to still keep him in the dark sir?"

"What did I told you about him the last time we talked agent Winston?" *Big D* asked

"Sir, you said that he was a little shit, that he had a Napoleonic Complex, and...that he...quote, didn't have shit on you. Unquote." Tom carefully responded

"Have I said anything to you to contradict that?"

"No sir" Tom answered him

"You know where I stand then agent Winston"

"Yes sir. It is very clear"

"Well, let's get to work then. Let's get moving on this ASAP"

"Yes sir" both Tom and Darren replied

They both exited Domenico's office as he was turning his television to CNN. Darren and Tom quickly walked towards the elevators. While waiting Darren abruptly asked "Tom, are you going to let Deputy Secretary Mallory know about the updates?"

With a surprised look on his face Tom quickly replied.

"Are you out of your freaking mind?"

"I take that as a no" Darren replied

They reached the first floor. They were just exiting the elevator when Tom let out a big sigh. He then started to rub the back of his neck. Darren sensed and saw the stress on Tom's face. He had been his closest friend during the entire 27 week academy training. Although he did not want to be too inquisitive he felt a duty to find out what was ailing Tom.

"Are you ok Tom?" Darren asked him "Too much to handle?"

"No Darren I'm ok. It's not our job that is bothering me, it's something more personal Darren. Things at home" Tom assured him.

"Everything ok with you and Lydia?"

"Oh yea. All is ok with us buddy. It's other stuff. Has to do more with our son Charlie."

"Is he sick?"inquired Darren

"No, not really. But…" Tom started saying while running his fingers thru his hair.

"Look Tom. I understand if you do not want to talk about your personal life but I am your friend and always here to talk ok?"

"Thanks Darren, I appreciate that. You are a good friend" Tom replied squeezing Darren's left shoulder.

"Come on, let's have a coffee and a snack at the cafeteria. My treat" Darren said.

They each ordered a coffee and a bagel sandwich. Tom drank his black while Darren had his with sugar and creamer. They sat down on a booth. Tom let out a deep breath and opened the conversation while Darren took a big bite of his bagel sandwich.

"As you know Darren, my son Charlie is an autistic child"

"Yes I am aware of that Tom. I commend you both for raising a great kid" said Darren while chomping on his sandwich. "If it was me I would not know how to deal with it. But you and Lydia had done a wonderful job raising him. Again, I commend you both my dear friend" Darren concluded while raising his cup of coffee, then taking a sip.

"Darren, as a good friend of mine I trust you. So, what I am about to tell you must stay between us. Understand?"

Darren drew a baffled look and then sat straight on the booth.

"Sure Tom. You are not about to die on me are you?"

"No I'm not Darren. I'm very healthy thank god. But I am serious. No word of this to anyone. And especially Lydia. If she finds out I told you this she will cut my balls off!" exclaimed Tom.

"I promise Tom. After all I do not want an agent backing me up without any balls. Got it? No balls? I'm sorry Tom" Darren responded trying not to laugh. "Go ahead. I'm listening"

"As I told you before it actually has to do with Charlie. A few weeks ago on the insistence from Lydia we decided to take Charlie to this psychiatrist. Lydia had been experiencing some unexplainable, weird situations while she was with Charlie."

"Like what?" asked Darren

"Feeling dizzy, weak, like in a trance, she says. Found herself saying words that were not actually hers. As if she was talking for someone else"

"Huh? What?"

"I know it sounds weird Darren but after visiting this well known psychiatrist I kind of experienced something unique myself too. Something I cannot explain" Tom confided

"You are freaking me out Tom. What is the name of this shrink. Are you sure she is as reputable as you think she is? And not some kind of witch doctor or scammer?"

"Yes I am sure. Well known author, written two books, studied at MIT and another Ivy League school. She is a neuropsychiatrist specializing on unexplainable events and conditions"

"What's her name?" Darren asked

"Abigail Lobowski" Tom answered him

Darren then took out a pen from inside his jacket and started scribbling her name.

"Lobo what? I am going to check her out" Darren assured him

"L-O-B-O-W-S-K-I. But there is no need Darren. She is legit, I assure you. Me and Lydia did a detailed background check on her and due diligence, as they say. After all, it's our son we are talking about"

"I believe you Tom. But I'm going to check her out nonetheless. *Abigail Lobowski*' Darren said as he finished writing on his pad. He put the pen and pad back inside his jacket.

"So, What happened inside her office?"

"Oh… she talked to us for sometime, asked Charlie a few questions, and then she did this… test"

"Test? What type of test?" asked Darren curiously

"She…um… recorded this video, with our consent of course. She then instructed Lydia and Charlie to look directly at me. Lydia put her hands on Charlie's shoulders and then almost immediately she started saying all these words"

"And?" Darren inquired further leaning forward to get closer to Tom.

"I… do not know exactly Darren. But I think Lydia was saying what I was thinking"

After a ten second pause Darren looked Tom straight into his eyes. "You kidding me right?"

"No I'm not Darren. I swear! It was as if she repeated what I was saying. Except I was not saying anything, I was thinking it!" Tom exclaimed pointing to his right temple.

"Hold on, hold your horses my friend! Are you telling me that you think Lydia has some type of telepathic, mind reading power? That she essentially read your mind inside that doctor's office?"

"Well, not actually her but, Charlie did" Tom said

"Now I'm really confused Tom" Darren replied

"Well, let me explain Darren. Apparently this doctor Lobowski is sure that Charlie has these telepathic ability and that he only transmits the thoughts from other persons to Lydia. Like, him being a transmitter and Lydia his receiver. At least that is the way she explained it to us"

"It must have been a trick Tom. Something inside her office, a magic trick of some kind to make you all think she was reading your mind"

"No, I don't think so Darren. I am sure Lydia was repeating was I was thinking. And this doctor is confident that Charlie is a very special, one of a kind autistic person with this capability"

"Hum… what else this shrink said?" inquired Darren

"She told Lydia that she needs to practice and control this special bond she now has with our son. Practice and patience, she told her"

"Wow! I know now why you looked so stressed out. The FBI academy graduation and now this weird shit"

"It's not weird shit Darren"

"No, no! I didn't meant it that way Tom!" replied Darren gesturing with both hands.

"I know you didn't my friend. I believe it's real. I believe Lydia is sensing this strong, special bond with Charlie. And I believe this power is getting stronger everyday"

"What makes you say that?" Darren asked him

"Something else happened after we returned from doctor Lobowski's office"

"Oh…there's more?" asked Darren inquisitively.

"After we pulled in into our driveway our neighbor's daughter was waiting there for us. She was wearing this tight sexy black dress with low cleavage. She wanted the attention. She is only sixteen and Lydia keeps telling me that she has a crush on me"

"Sixteen! Oh yeah!" Darren called out. "Tom, you dirty dog!"

"It's not like that Darren. Charlie has a crush on her of course. She is a beautiful girl and Lydia clearly noticed what she was up to.

Anyways, I went inside the house while her and Charlie were talking to her. Without Lydia noticing I kept looking outside. I then saw Lydia whispered something into her ear. And then, all of a sudden, Mayra, that's the girls name, turned away and ran like she had seen the devil herself. She almost fell on the ground"

Darren then whispered to Tom "Do you think Lydia told her to stay the fuck away from her husband?"

"Something like that. But I suspect she used the same method she used while at doctor Lobowski's office" Tom replied back

"You mean, she read her thoughts too?" asked Darren

"Yes I do. And I think she really enjoyed it. Especially when she now feels that strong and very special bond with our son Charlie"

"Did you say anything to her afterwards?"

"No. I just went to the kitchen pretending to look for something to eat"

Darren put both of his elbows on the table holding tightly his cup of coffee. He took another sip and then said "Holy shit Tom! That is a hell of a story buddy"

"It is, isn't it?" answered Tom taking a sip of his too.

That same night Darren could not forget that dialogue with Tom at the cafeteria. Deliberations ran thru his mind. Not only Tom's recent chat but Domenico's request and briefings concerning the Galapagos Islands status. He could not sleep, as he fumbled with the bed sheets and moved from side to side almost all night. He could not forget that peculiar talk with Tom. And, at the same time neither Domenico's words during their last meeting. Especially the ones referring to *reading their minds*; when talking about Perchenko and Melancón. But Darren was torn apart between the promise he had made to his friend Tom Winston and his duty as an FBI agent sworn in to safeguard and defend his country. At about two in the morning his body gave up. His alarm woke him up at exactly seven that morning. He laid on his bed trying to envision the *what ifs* and the consequences of his future actions. Should he do it or not? Should he be quiet about the whole thing or betray his best friend? The friend that had helped him so much during those hard days at the FBI Academy. He pondered hard. He deliberated very hard. Darren finally sat on the side of his bed and although hesitant about it, picked up his cell phone. He then dialed Big D's phone number.

"Good morning agent Johnson. Miss me already?" Domenico answered

"Good morning to you sir." He loathed at first then added "I... need to talk to you about something important sir"

Even after making that phone call to Domenico it would be almost forty eight hours before Darren decided to stop by his office. He was still indecisive after the call but he finally was convinced that he was doing the just thing. After stopping at his office Darren told him all about his talk with Tom at the cafeteria. Not only that but Darren also proceeded to present Domenico with a plan that could resolve their lack of information regarding Perchenko and Melancón. Big D was really impressed with this new, fresh presentation and Darren's attitude towards solving the problem. "You will go far at the agency, son" Domenico started saying "with this impressive attitude" he continued, "you will climb the ladder in no time" he concluded.

"Yes sir!" Darren replied with a slight smile

So they both devised a plan, without Tom of course, that would hopefully tell the intel community what the Presidents of Russia and Ecuador were up to. Good or bad they needed to find out as soon as possible. They gave their newly planned mission a name: *Operation Carondelet.*

After Darren presented his idea to Domenico, Domenico sat down on his desk and wrote himself a note. It said; 'pay visit to doctor Lobowski'

"Sir, you don't think our plan is too far fetched?" asked Darren

"No. I don't think it is agent Johnson. This might just work. It is a little bit risky but, we do not have many other options, do we? And the

Russian ships will be in Ecuadorian waters in about two weeks. Time is not on our side son"

"So, what next sir?" Darren asked

"Let me pay a visit to this doctor Lobowski and find out what she actually knows" Big D responded crossing his arms in front of him.

8

Admiral Alexander Abramov was in his late fifties, well fit and for this reason probably did look younger than his age. He had a square jaw, steely blue eyes, and sporting a crew cut. Dressed in his immaculate Russian Navy uniform he wore all of his medals proudly after serving over twenty eight years on the Russian Navy. He sat straight as an arrow on his red leather chair and punched a button on his desk phone.

"Connect me to the President" he asked in a deep voice

"Yes Admiral Abramov. Right away" a female voice answered

After about a fifteen second wait President Perchenko's voice came up on the speaker phone.

"Hello Admiral Abramov. All running as scheduled I suppose?"

"Yes Mr President. Just wanted to report that the 43rd Missile Division is on its way Mr. President" Abramov answered him

"Good to hear Admiral. How long before they reach destination?" Perchenko asked

"Ten to twelve days assuming they do not encounter any bad weather"

"And, as we talked earlier Admiral, I want maximum exposure from the news. Make sure that enough is leaked to the media"

"Yes Mr President. That should not be hard to do. It will be like feeding raw fish to hungry sharks sir" Abramov replied

"Good! I will be meeting again with our Ecuadorian friend soon. I want to make sure that all is in place for our ships to enter the Archipielago. In the meantime Admiral, let me know of any problems our ship division may encounter"

"Understood Mr. President. I will keep you posted" Abramov replied

"Happy sailing Admiral Abramov" said Perchenko

"Thank you Mr. President. For the motherland!" exclaimed Admiral Abramov

"For the motherland Admiral Abramov! Goodbye" Perchenko said as he ended the call

The Russian 43rd Missile Ship Division consisting of an aircraft carrier, two battlecruisers, a Guards Missile Cruiser, and a Gorshkov class frigate officially started sail that day. Their destination; the Galapagos Islands Archipelago, approximately eight hundred fifty nautical miles southeast of the Panama Canal. Admiral Abramov stood up from his red leather chair. He picked up a shot glass from a small bar behind his desk and filled it with the premier vodka he always enjoyed. After drinking it he carefully put he shot glass back on his bar. He then clasped his hands behind his back and stared at the map of Russia spread over the wall.

"God help us all!" he exclaimed

FBI agent Dolan Domenico arrived at doctor's Lobowski's office at three fifteen in the afternoon. He was driving an official black Ford sedan vehicle and was squinting his eyes as he tried to look at the building number. It was an unusual warm, sunny day in Fredericksburg. He eventually found the correct building at the Eastwood Medical Plaza complex.

"Ok here we go" he said as he closed the car door "all right doctor, let's see what you have for me"

He proceeded to the elevators and pressed the button for the fouth floor. As soon as he entered doctor Lobowski's suite her assistant Ma greeted him with her wide smile.

"Hello, may I help you?" she asked in her strong accent

"Yes Miss. I have an appointment with doctor Lobowski at three thirty"

"May I ask your name sir?" she asked

"My last name is Domenico. Agent Domenico" Big D answered as he pulled his FBI credentials and showed her.

"Oh!...ok. I will let her know you are here agent"

"Thank you Miss" Domenico replied as he sat on one of the reception chairs. He looked around the office. He was about to pick up a National Geographic magazine when Ma interrupted him.

"The doctor can see you now agent" said Ma

Doctor Lobowski was standing by her office door and she extended her hand to Domenico. Big D was startled by her small figure. He realized she was not even five feet tall.

"Glad to meet you doctor Lobowski" Domenico said shaking her small hand.

"Nice to meet you too agent Domenico" the doctor replied "please sit down" she concluded as she closed the door behind her.

"Thank you for letting me see you doctor. Here are my credentials" Big D answered while showing his FBI badge to doctor Lobowski.

"Well, agent Domenico, how can I help you today? Is not everyday I get a visit from a federal agent" Lobowski said raising her eyebrows "Am I in trouble?"

"No, nothing like that doctor. I'm interested in finding information about a patient you are treating. His name is Charles Winston. I understand he is an autistic person."

"And,...may I ask agent Domenico...how do you know I am treating this patient? What are your sources"?

"Very reliable sources doctor. Also, his father happens to work for the agency as a new FBI agent, by the way"

"Really?" asked doctor Lobowski "Small world isn't it?"

"Yes it is doctor. Now, can I ask you when was the last visit with the Winston family?" Domenico inquired

Doctor Lobowski leaned forward and clasped her hands on top of her desk.

"You know I cannot tell you that... agent Domenico. That is... confidential... between doctor and her patient"

"Understand doctor. But can you tell me at least what was discussed in general during these meetings?" Big D asked again

"Now...agent Domenico...why such and interest...in a young thirteen year old...autistic child, may I ask?" doctor Lobowski asked breaking her sentence as usual.

"That is confidential too doctor. Sorry, need to know only" he answered her.

"You have to be kidding me. Really?"

"Let's just say doctor that it is a matter of national security."

"And if I refuse to give you any information?"

Big D pulled his chair closer to doctor Lobowski's desk and then stared directly at her. He then put both arms on top of her desk.

"Look doctor" Domenico started in a low tone of voice "of course you do not have to give me any information right now. But it would not be pretty serving you with a search warrant from the FBI in front of one of your patients, would it? I mean, you have a reputation to protect, I'm sure"

"Do the Winstons know that you are here?"

"No they do not doctor. And we can keep it that way." Domenico responded

Doctor Lobowski realized she did not have any other choice but to cooperate with Domenico. Perhaps, she could bend the truth a little, give him a slice of the pie, instead of the whole pie, she thought.

"What do you want to know agent Domenico?" she asked somewhat concerned.

"For starters. How many sessions have you done so far with the Winstons?"

"Three so far" doctor Lobowski said as he scribbled on his notepad.

"Doctor, can you tell me what was the reason the Winstons brought their son to see you?"

"Well...Mrs. Winston was not feeling well lately..."

"You said Mrs. Winston. Lydia Winston?" Domenico interrupted her

"Yes, her." Lobowski answered reluctantly

"But I thought her son Charles was your patient, not her"

"Let's say it has...to do... with both?"

"With both you say"

"Yes, with both"

"In what way doctor. Can you explain in more detail please?" asked Domenico curiously

Doctor Lobowski cleared her throat before before responding to Domenico "We can say agent Domenico; that they share a very special...mother and son relationship. A very special connection... that... some parents of autistic children do not usually have."

"A connection, hum...and by that doctor, do you happen to be referring to some type of telepathic link by any chance, or...mind reading capacity doctor Lobowski?"

"I see that you have done your homework. Your source must be... well connected to the Winston family. Why do you need me then?"

"Yes I still need you doc. I need every detail of Charles Winston potential. I understand you graduated with a degree from Stanford and MIT. In your professional opinion doctor Lobowski, have you seen anyone like Charles Winston before?"

"No I have not..." answered Lobowski

"And, how many years have you been practicing as a neuropsychiatrist?"

"For twenty five years"

Domenico crossed his arms in front of his chest and then asked doctor Loboswski. "What makes him so special doctor?"

"He is different..." answered the doctor

"How doctor, in which way?" Domenico inquired

Doctor Lobowski started rubbing her hands before she answered Big D "he is...more...I would say...aware of his abilities. He knows how to control it, much more focused"

"You mean reading other people's minds"

"You make him sound like he is a freak agent Domenico...or some kind...of street magician. Well, he is not sir. He has a very special gift... that he can use for the good of humanity"

"And, in your opinion doc, this...gift that you say he has, will it get stronger or weaker as he gets older?" asked Big D

"It will never get weaker agent Domenico. As he gets older... and more mature... and knows how to control it,... his telepathic powers will only get much stronger. I assure you of that" Lobowski replied slightly raising her voice.

Out of the corner of his eye Domenico noticed a camera on a tripod that was leaning on its side by a bookcase.

"Doctor Lobowski"he started "by any chance, have you recorded any videos of your sessions with the Winstons?"

"No I have not" she quickly responded

"Are you sure about that doc?"

"I'm sure. I do not have a reason to lie. Especially to a federal agent"

"Yeah, I guess you don't doctor. And, one more question doctor. Do you think Charles Winston is the only autistic person with these capabilities or, do you think there might be more like him around the world?"

"He is the only one I've treated. But to answer your question...yes... there is a strong possibility that there may be more like him. Maybe... afraid to come out of the woods...as they say. Agent Domenico... I have a four fifteen appointment with another patient. Are we done here?" doctor Lobowski said standing up.

"Oh...sure doc. Don't want to hold you up" Domenico said as he reached into his shirt pocket and handed doctor Lobowski his business card.

"Doctor, if you can think of anything else other that we have discussed here today, anything out of the ordinary about the Winstons sessions please give me a call anytime"

"I sure will agent Domenico. I sure will" said Lobowski

Domenico stood up and extended his hand to doctor Lobowski.

"It was a pleasure to meet you doctor" he told her

"The pleasure was mine agent Domenico"Lobowski replied

Domenico started walking towards the door when doctor Lobowski asked him "agent Domenico?"

Dolan Domenico stopped and looked back at her.

"Just wanted to let you know that everything *is* 'out of the ordinary' during Charlie's sessions!" she exclaimed.

"Thanks for letting me know doc" Domenico said before leaving her office.

As soon as Domenico got inside his car he made a call on his cell phone. "Yes sir" he started saying "I need a search warrant for a doctor by the name of Abigail Lobowski as soon as possible. The address is 3282 Pinewood Boulevard, suite 410, at the Eastwood Medical Plaza."

After ending the call he laid back on the backseat, and then ran his fingers thru his hair. He then took a long breath.

"Charlie...what's on your mind Charlie Winston?" he asked himself

9

It wasn't long before it was all over the news and social media channels and sites. The story about the Russian Navy 43rd Missile Ship Division sailing towards Central and South American waters to join more ships already off the coast of Ecuador spread quickly like a chronic disease creating despair, confusion, and panic among American households. Questions and rumors were everywhere especially on social media. Was the United States facing another Cuban Missile crisis? What was the purpose of the Russian Navy increasing number of ships and strong military presence of the central and south american waters? Were the Russians planning and invasion of the United States thru the west coast? Were they preparing to block the Panama Canal and choke the busiest and most transited maritime trade waterway in the world? Out of all of these rumors proliferating all over the world the most outrageous of course was that of the Russians planning and outright invasion thru the western United States forcing the state of California to declare a state of emergency; although there was absolutely no proof of such a future calamity from either the federal government or intelligence agencies.

But the governor of California and local governmental agencies had decided not to take a chance declaring the state of emergency and warning residents to be prepared for a possible Russian or even

Chinese invasion thru the California coast. About three days after the emergency declaration eighty five percent of all weapons and ammunition was sold out across all of the gun shops and retail stores across the state. Pure chaos, just as Domenico had predicted, and just what the Russians wanted. And, as general Alexander Abramov so eloquently had stated earlier, the feeding frenzy had just commenced.

"What in the hell is going on hun?" Lydia asked Tom as she watched the breaking news.

"Just rumors Lydia, don't worry about it babe" he answered her

"But California just declared a state of emergency Tom. Do you think all of this is just rumors?"

Tom glanced at the television then turned to Lydia "Yes I do honey, I really do" Tom tried to convince her. She had enough on her plate to worry about all of these international political crises, he thought.

"Well, have to drop Charlie at school. Have a good day at the field office hun" said Lydia

"Thanks babe. You have a good day too"

"Love you" Lydia answered giving Tom a light kiss

"You ready Charlie?" Lydia yelled from downstairs. Charlie came running downstairs straight to the front door.

"Love you buddy. Have a great day at school champ" Tom said to Charlie.

"Love you dad. Goodbye" Charlie responded but without looking back at Tom. After Lydia closed the front door behind her Tom turned up the volume on the television. A wide red label with white lettering ran across the bottom of the Fox News channel. Tom tried to read the message as it scrolled from right to left across the screen. It read: *reliable sources confirm more Russian Navy ships getting closer to Central American waters. World intelligence unknown of Russian intentions. Defense Secretary Michael Donovan scheduled to have a briefing at the Department of Defense at 5:00 PM eastern time. More to follow.*

"Jesus Christ! Here we go!" Tom cried out

Meanwhile at his office Domenico was just answering a call from his source Simon. Simon had immediately called Big D as soon as the breaking news hit the morning channels.

"Yes I know sir. It's a feeding frenzy out there" said Big D "I was afraid this would happen" he added

"I agree. And our nemesis Perchenko did not waste any time spreading the rumors" responded Simon. They were on a secure line and Simon's voice was obviously altered.

"I wonder why so fast? What does he gain by spreading hearsay so quick?" asked Domenico

"I'm sure he has a reason agent Domenico. We do not have too much time left to find the answer, and for this reason we may have to activate Operation Carondelet ahead of time" Simon replied

"How much early sir?"

"Within seventy two hours. The President is ready to encounter those Russian ships face to face if necessary" Simon answered

"Seventy two hours…"Domenico started saying as he took a glance outside his office window. "And, how…exactly do you want us to proceed sir?" he asked

"We must acquire the asset" Simon answered him

After Simon said this Domenico went silent for about ten seconds while still staring thru his office window.

"Agent Domenico, are you still there?" Simon demanded

"Yes sir. I'm still here sir" Big D answered

"Do you understand what I just said Domenico?"

"Yes sir. Clearly. I understand"

"We must take the asset and bring it to a secure location. We need to know as soon as possible the asset's potential before we can proceed further with Operation Carondelet" Simon explained

"Got it sir"

"Do you need any help from our friends at the CIA?" Simon asked Domenico

"No sir. We can handle it" Domenico answered quickly

"Good" Simon replied "Get your team together agent Domenico. You have seventy two hours before the President decides to send our ships to the Panama Canal to intercept the Russian Navy"

"Understood sir" Domenico assured him

"I will call you back again in exactly twenty four hours to see how the operation is proceeding" said Simon

"Yes sir. I will have a report by then" Big D replied

"Good luck agent Domenico"

"Thank you Simon"

Big D carefully placed the phone back on his desk. He rubbed his tired eyes, sighed and placed a call from another cell phone to agent Darren Johnson. As soon as he answered Domenico said to him "the game is on agent Johnson"

United States Secretary of Defense Michael Donovan gave a briefing at precisely five in the evening inside the press room at the Pentagon. He described in detail how the Russian Navy was accumulating a surprisingly forceful presence in central and south american waters and then proceeded to answer many questions from reporters packed inside the newsroom. Domenico was following closely the fast moving events as he and Darren Johnson talked inside his office.

"So, we are cleared to proceed sir?" asked Darren

"Yes we are son" Domenico answered "things are moving fast so we must acquire the asset as soon as we can agent Johnson"

"And where is the asset going to be secured sir?" inquired Darren

"In a secret location about one hundred miles north of the city of Las Vegas. Smack in the middle of the freaking desert" Big D answered him.

"What time?"

"Asset is to be acquired at around ten hundred hours tomorrow. A group of world experts will be waiting at the secret location for evaluation. After their report then we will proceed as they suggest" explained Domenico

"Understand sir" said Darren

The next day as usual Lydia dropped Charlie at his special school in Fredericksburg. She gave him a firm motherly hug, a kiss on his forehead, and told him as always how much she loved him. Charlie quickly ran to his room eager to meet his other classmates. Lydia then proceeded to do a few chores. At around four in the afternoon she was in front of Charlie's school waiting to pick him up. Around four thirty in the afternoon Tom received a call from Lydia. She was breathing hard, very upset, and screaming.

"Oh my God Tom!" she started yelling to Tom thru her cell phone

"Are you ok Lydia? What is going on? Are you hurt honey?" Tom asked her distraught. He could feel the panic on her voice

"I'm fine Tom. It's Charlie!" she yelled back at Tom

"What about Charlie Lydia?" Tom asked her

"I came to pick him up from school. He is not here Tom! He is missing! Our son is missing Tom! Someone else picked him up from school! Oh my God Tom! Where is Charlie?!" Lydia continued yelling hysterically on her phone.

10

"Can you think of anyone, anyone at all that would want to hurt your family Mr. Winston, Mrs. Winston?" the cop asked Tom and Lydia

"No! Of course not officer!" Tom answered him

"Any grudges with any of your co workers, promotions, money owed, possible blackmail...anything like that?" the officer asked again

"My wife is a stay at home mom because of our son's condition. I just graduated from the FBI Academy and during our training we were like a close knit family. I could not think of anyone trying to hurt our family. And, my assignment at my new field office is going fine"

The Fredericksburg Police had arrived at their house around five thirty in the evening after Lydia and Tom had reported Charlie missing.

"Any financial problems Mr. Winston?" the other officer asked

"No. None. We are doing fine too in that department. This does not make any sense. Why would anyone want to kidnap our son officer?" Tom asked curiously

"Don't really know Mr. Winston. Sometimes we miss the most obvious clues" the police officer responded

The police officers had been at their residence for almost an hour now asking questions, some of them very personal. Tom was not comfortable answering them but knew that he had to answer them if they wanted to know what had happened to Charlie. Lydia was at the bottom of the stairs sitting on the first step. She was holding tight to one of Charlie's shirts and a picture of him, both items she had picked up from Charlie's room. She was sobbing and shaking as she squeezed Charlie's shirt against her chest.

"Officers, if you don't mind" Tom started saying as he took a glance at Lydia. "I need to take care of my wife. She is very upset as you can see"

"Yes. Of course Mr. Winston. We will let you and your wife rest. You both have been thru enough today. We have Charlie's picture. We will enter it into our database as soon as we get to our precinct. A detective will be in contact with both of you tomorrow morning" the officer said to Tom

"Thank you officers" Tom replied

"You are welcome sir. Have a good evening"

As soon as the police officers left Tom kneeled in front of Lydia. She was holding to Charlie's shirt tightly against her chest, saying nothing, staring at the floor.

"Lydia, honey. Can you talk to me? Please?" Tom asked her. But no answer from Lydia.

"Honey, do you want me to bring you something to relax, to help you sleep tonight?" Tom asked her again

Lydia slightly swung her head side to side to let Tom know she did not want anything. Tom gently pulled up Lydia's chin and looked straight into her eyes.

"We will find Charlie Lydia. I promise you. We will get our son back" Tom assured her

All of a sudden Lydia grabbed him, pulled Tom closer to her and started crying even louder.

"Who took Charlie Tom? Where is Charlie? Where is my Charlie?" Lydia screamed as she wrapped her arms around Tom and held tight to Charlie's shirt on her left hand and to his picture on the right. Tom could feel her wet cheek against his. Her fresh tears joining his.

He suddenly remembered the last time, a time it was so sad for him, he could not contain back his tears. It was at his father's funeral. Now he was shedding tears for his son. His only son. His teenage son who so badly needed them. He could not wrap around his head who would want to take Charlie. It sure was not because of money, as they were not wealthy. Was this some kind of sick joke? Some terrorist plot against the Agency? Human trafficking? Would they be asking for ransom money later? All types of scenarios ran thru his mind concerning Charlie's abduction, but for now he had to be strong and concentrate on taking care of Lydia. He did not want to lose her too. He was going to use all of the resources at his disposal, including the Agency's, to bring his son back home.

The luxurious Gulfstream G280 private jet landed at McCarran International Airport in Las Vegas. As it taxied to a private terminal any of the thousands of tourists walking up and down the Las Vegas Strip would easily assume it was carrying someone famous, very wealthy, or a high roller being a guest at one of the casinos. But that was not the case. Inside, the passengers were none of these. A total of seven travelers exited the private jet boarding directly into two black Cadillac Escalades. They were all immediately transported less than one mile away to a nearby hangar where the Blackhawk helicopter blades were already turning and waiting for them. The newly arrived fliers then boarded the Blackhawk heading north towards the Nevada desert. It was sunset, and the combination of the sun and scattered clouds gave the sky of the city of lights the usual orange color as the silhouette of the helicopter on the foreground became smaller. It was heading northwest, carrying all of them, to the secured location.

Secured Location: Nevada desert, 115 miles northwest of Las Vegas

It was building 911, named after the biggest terrorist attack on U.S. soil, where the group of seven was taken. Three world renowned neuroscientists, FBI agents Domenico and Johnson, doctor Lobowski, and the asset itself, Charles Winston. The building was painted a faint white color to minimize the desert heat absorption, with few windows, built out of concrete. The numbers 911 where located in the upper left hand corner of the building in bright black colors. No other special signs or markings were around the building, inconspicuously constructed in the middle of the Nevada desert one hundred fifteen miles northwest from the city of Las Vegas. A few hundred feet before the nine eleven building was a security gate with two armed guards dressed in camel colored camouflage uniforms. Each guard wore a nine millimeter handgun around their waists and a semi automatic gun on their shoulders. The gate was manned twenty four hours. The group of seven advanced to the gate in a white van with dark tinted windows before it was stopped by one of the heavy armed guards. The driver of the van opened his window.

"Credentials please?" the guard asked

Agent Domenico was on the front passenger seat and quickly showed his badge and credentials to the guard. Agent Johnson followed showing his. Domenico then handled the guard a set of classified documents.

"We are here with the asset along with the three neuroscientists and doctor Lobowski" Domenico explained

The guard meticulously examined the documents and then took a close look at all of the passengers. After he was convinced all was in order he gave a sign to the other guard.

"They are all clear. They can proceed" he yelled to the other guard by the gate

The gate opened and the white van advanced to the nine eleven structure only entrance where a tall, slender woman in her early forties with blondish hair awaited for them. She greeted Domenico extending her right hand.

"Welcome agent Domenico. We have been waiting for you and your group. My name is Helen Machado. I am the general manager of building nine eleven" she said to Domenico

"Nice to meet you Helen. This is agent Darren Johnson. And these are doctors Mendez, Sheridan, Henderson, and doctor Lobowski" he answered pointing to the group

"Nice to meet you all" replied Helen

"And, this is Charlie" Domenico said

"Well, hello Charlie" Helen started saying while extending her hand to him. "We have heard great things about you Charlie"

Charlie did not shake her hand or answered her.

"Well, great to meet you Charlie" she said withdrawing her hand away from Charlie "please follow me"

The all walked along a narrow corridor. Domenico was in front of the group with Helen by his side while doctor Lobowski followed behind them holding Charlie's hand. The three neuroscientists strolled behind her. They turned right where they were multiple guest rooms on both sides of the hallway.

"They are plenty of rooms here if you all want to refresh if you want" Helen said with a smile

"Thank you Helen. It won't take us long. We must start examining the asset as soon as we can" Domenico said

"I understand agent Domenico. I will be waiting at the examination room"

Helen then walked away and turned right at the end of the hallway.

Domenico turned towards doctor Lobowski and said to her "ready to have a talk with him?" he asked her

"As ready as I can be" doctor Lobowski answered him

"Ok. Good. We will meet here again in exactly one hour" Domenico instructed while looking at his watch.

Doctors Mendez, Sheridan, and Henderson went inside one room. Darren went inside another one leaving the door open for Domenico. Doctor Lobowski was opening her room door when she suddenly turned back and said to Domenico "I hope that you are doing the right thing" she said

Domenico looked back at her and replied "I hope I am too doc. I hope I am"

Doctor Lobowski went inside her room with Charlie. It was very simple, with cheap furniture, small shower and toilet room, and a small five cup coffee maker. Doctor Lobowski checked the small coffee filters laying on the cheap desk. A small layer of dust flew up into the air after she shook some of them. "Cheap bastards!" she exclaimed

Charlie sat on the desk chair right away while doctor Lobowski sat at the end of the bed facing him.

"Charlie, do you know why we are here?" she asked him

"We are going to play a game. Then we are going to go to Disney World" he replied

"That's right. If you win this...game...then we can take you...to Disney World. As you always wanted"

"Yes. Where is my mom? I want to see my mom. Where is she? Where is my mommy? Charlie asked repeatedly

"She will be here soon Charlie. And then...you and your mom... and your dad...will be going together" she assured Charlie

"Are you coming with us?"

"No I can't Charlie. But...I will be here...helping you to win the game, ok?" the doctor said

"Ok" Charlie replied staring at the floor

"Good boy Charlie. I know you will win the game" doctor Lobowski assured Charlie.

She really hated to be a part of Operation Carondelet. But after the search warrant was issued her office was raided by the FBI taking all of the videos she had taken with the Winston family. Agent Domenico then threaten her with jail time for lying to him and hiding evidence. She did not have any choice but to cooperate with the FBI and Domenico. She could not afford to throw away her life long career. Domenico made a deal with her. She would be close to Charlie during the examinations of his potentials as Charlie had won her trust during their sessions at her office. In exchange, she would have her practice back without any worries of legal repercussions against her.

One hour later as Domenico had instructed they all met back in the hallway. They walked to a set of double doors with a red sign and white letters that read *Authorized Personnel Only!*. Domenico pressed his right index finger into a small scanner and a light click was heard. He then pushed the door open and the group of seven went inside. Helen was already there waiting for them.

"Hello again you'all" she said in her Texan accent "ready to begin?"

"Yes we are" Domenico answered her

The room looked more like an interrogation room, four hundred square feet at the most, with three tall glass window enclosures. At the other side of the windows Charlie was sitting in front of a table with doctor Lobowski by his side. The three neuroscientists were on the other side of the table. Doctor Henderson and Sheridan were sitting opposite Charlie while doctor Mendez was standing behind them. Domenico, Darren, and Helen stood on the other side of the windows attentively looking at all of them when one of the doctors broke the silence and greeted Charlie.

"Hello Charlie. My name is doctor Henderson. These are doctor Sheridan and doctor Mendez. Charlie, can you tell us your full name please?"

"Charles Winston" replied Charlie while staring at the table

"And, how old are you Charlie?"

"Thirteen"

"Wow. Thirteen. I have a daughter who is also thirteen. Here, do you want to see her picture?" doctor Henderson asked him reaching into his back pocket for his wallet.

"No" Charlie quickly answered him

"Oh...ok. That's fine Charlie. Charlie, do you play sports?"

"No"

"Do you like any sports, video games?"

"I like the MMA, martial arts boxing" Charlie responded with his head still down

"Really? What do you like about it?"

Meanwhile, at the other side of the glass Domenico was getting frustrated with doctor Henderson's line of questioning.

"What is he doing?" Domenico whispered

"I guess he is trying to break the ice sir" Darren said

Charlie answered doctor Henderson's last question "I like it when they kick each other on their faces and blood comes out"

After Charlie said this all three doctors started laughing hard at Charlie's response.

"Kicking their faces, ha, ha ha...! That is funny Charlie!" doctor Henderson injected

Abruptly, Charlie raised his head, gave a serious look to doctor Henderson and yelled "MMA is a serious sport! And I like it! Why are you making fun of it?"

The room went completely silent. Doctor Lobowski looked back at agent Domenico thru the glass windows for a few seconds. Doctor Henderson stopped laughing as well as his two other colleagues. He cleared his throat before he addressed Charlie again.

"Sorry Charlie" he started saying "I didn't mean it that way. We were not...making fun of your favorite sport Charlie. Ok?"

Charlie clearly looked upset. Doctor Lobowski put her hand softly on one of his shoulders and then whispered to Charlie "are you ok Charlie?"

"Yes" Charlie answered her still staring at doctor Henderson. Doctor Lobowski then gave a nod to doctor Henderson to continue.

Doctor Henderson cleared his throat a second time and then proceeded to unbutton the top of his perfectly ironed white shirt.

"Charlie, do you know why we are here with you?" he asked

"Yes" Charlie answered looking back at doctor Lobowski "she told me. We are playing a game and then we will go to Disney World"

"Yes we are Charlie. As soon as we are done with the game you can reunite with your parents" doctor Henderson said

Doctor Henderson then continued "Charlie, to start the game, if you don't mind, can doctor Mendez stand right behind you?"

Charlie hesitated at first, and the said "yes, he can"

Doctor Mendez walked around the table and stood behind Charlie. Doctor Henderson cleared his throat once again and said to Charlie "Charlie, can doctor Mendez put his hands on top of your shoulders?" Charlie looked back at doctor Mendez and nodded yes. Doctor Mendez then proceeded to put both of his hands firmly on Charlie's shoulders. His hands were shaking a bit, he felt somewhat uneasy.

Doctor Lobowski then turned to Charlie and said to him "Charlie, just...remember...the first time you...and your parents visited my office. Remember? Remember the way you *listened* ... to your dad. We want you to concentrate real hard... and *listen* the same way you did to your dad but to doctor Henderson this time. Do you understand Charlie?"

"Yes" Charlie simply responded

Charlie stared at doctor Henderson for a few seconds. He then saw a smirk come to doctor Henderson's face as if mocking Charlie. Charlie continued fixated on the doctor's face. He could *listen* to him now. He could clearly hear his voice although doctor Henderson's lips were not moving.

"Ha, ha, ha, ha...ok kid, let's see if you are the real thing as they said. I believe you are just a farce. I've seen many like you. Trying to pretend to have all of these special powers. Ha! I personally think you are playing all of us. And you MMA story, oh my God! That was really funny! What a joke. That's not even a real sport you little shit. You better get back to your mommy before you start crying!"

After Charlie finished *listening* to doctor Henderson, without any warning, doctor Mendez's head started to bend backwards as if it was being pulled by another being. His breathing started to get heavier and faster and his eyes started to roll back. He suddenly started shaking. Charlie's eyes were strictly focused on doctor Henderson. Doctor Mendez head continued to stretch back until it was almost at a ninety degree angle.

"What is going on?" Domenico asked distraught

"Don't know boss" Darren said somewhat baffled

"It's hot in here!" Doctor Henderson yelled all of a sudden "I'm sweating like crazy!" he hollered again

His perfectly ironed white shirt was now all full of sweat. Charlie was not about to let the doctor make fun of him or his mother. Next, doctor Mendez started to shake uncontrollably at the same time that it looked like his neck was about to snap from his body. Doctor Henderson's shirt was now completely cover with his sweat, but within seconds, blood started to pour out of doctor Henderson's pores. Patches of red started to spread all over his white shirt.

"What the hell is happening?" Darren screamed

"What in God's name...!" Helen yelled

Blood continued to ooze from the doctor's pores and his shirt continued to soak it until it was all red. Charlie then *heard* doctor Henderson's plea in spite of the fact that he was not talking at all.

"Please, please stop! I'm sorry! Charlie could *hear* him say.

Domenico instantly pressed the button on the microphone that connected the two rooms and yelled to doctor Lobowski.

"Doctor Lobowski! Tell him to stop! Now!"

Doctor Lobowski glanced at doctor Mendez's neck. His head and neck were almost horizontal to his body at the same time that doctor Henderson's shirt was saturated in his own blood. He yelled at Charlie to stop but Charlie's eyes were still obsessed with doctor Henderson. She yelled louder, then louder, then much louder "Charlie! Stop!"

After screaming at Charlie for a third time doctor Mendez's body went limp, fell on top of doctor Lobowski who in turn hit the floor hard with her head. Doctor Henderson's body fell backwards on his chair splattering blood all over the floor. Helen, the administrator for the nine eleven building started screaming hysterically. Domenico tried to take control of the situation.

"Helen, Helen, listen! We need the medics here now! Call the medics!" Domenico yelled to her. He then barged into the other side of the room where he found doctor Lobowski laying on the floor, doctor Mendez barely breathing, and doctor Henderson laying on a pool of his own blood. He first checked on doctor Lobowski. She was rubbing the back of her head.

"Are you ok doc?" He asked her while he helped her off the floor.

"Yes, I'm fine Domenico" she moaned still rubbing the back of her head. "But I'm not sure about these two" she concluded referring to doctors Henderson and Mendez.

Dolan Domenico got closer to doctor Mendez who was breathing, but erratically. Darren Johnson meanwhile checked on doctor Henderson's condition. He approached him and started to check his pulse on his neck.

"I got a pulse sir, but faint" Darren said

"Ok. We must evacuate them to a hospital now!" demanded agent Domenico

"Got it sir!"Darren agreed at the same time he ran to the other side of the room.

"Where are the medics Miss Machado?" Darren asked

"They should be here any minute" Helen answered still shaking

"Where is doctor Sheridan?" asked Domenico to all

"I think he he got spooked and ran away" said doctor Lobowski

Domenico then took a look at Charlie. He was still sitting calmly on his chair, staring at where doctor Henderson had been seating. He did not say anything, his palms firmly on the table. Staring straight ahead Charlie said softly "Where is my mom? I want to see my mom"

The medic team arrived and rushed inside the room

"In here!" Domenico yelled waving them to the other side of the glass. The medics immediately started attending doctor Mendez and doctor Henderson. Dolan and Darren stared at each other. Darren sighed and then said "What now sir?" he asked

""I must call Simon and give him a report" said Domenico

On the other side of the phone line Simon was clearly not happy.

"What the fuck Dolan? Is the asset safe?" Simon asked

"Yes sir. The asset was not compromised sir. But two of the neuroscientists were hurt, one badly. The third one freaked out and ran away from the room" Domenico explained to Simon

"Where is the asset now Dolan?"

"It is secured inside building nine eleven"

"Well, find this dipshit doctor and make sure he does not talk to anybody"

"We will sir. The guards are looking for him right now. He can't go far" Domenico assured him

"Good. Let's get this mess cleaned up and I will be in touch with you again soon"

"Yes sir, we will"

"I will brief the President and see what he decides to do next" said Simon

"Understood sir" Domenico responded before he hung up

"He is not happy...huh?" said Darren

"Nope" Domenico responded as he took out a cigarette. He had quit many years ago but today he really needed one. Him and Darren had gone outside for much needed fresh air. The front door of building nine eleven slowly opened and the small figure of doctor Lobowski came into view.

"How is he doctor?" Domenico asked her

"He is doing fine. He is watching his martial arts fights on the tv. He keeps asking about his mother" the doctor answered

"And the doctors?"

"They were taken on the helicopter to a Las Vegas Hospital"

"Good. Great!" Domenico said with a sigh of relief. "What happened in there doc? Never seen anything like it. And believe me, I've seen some crazy shit in my lifetime" he finished saying

"Well...like I told you before agent Domenico...his powers will get stronger...as he knows how to control them. It looks to me that one of your neuroscientists really...pissed him off. If I was you...I would not bet against him" doctor Lobowski explained

"Any ideas doc?" asked Domenico taking a puff of his smoke

"I think you only have half of the puzzle"

"What do you mean doc?" Domenico asked curiously

"What I mean is...do not work against Charlie...but...work *with* Charlie. The only way you are going to work in Charlie's favor...is for you to get the other side of the puzzle. The person...he trusts most in this world, the receiver of his thoughts...his mother"

"His mother? For God's sake doc. You want me to get his mother involved in this turmoil after we have done?"

Doctor Lobowski gave Domenico a puzzled stare and replied to him "We? What do you mean we? As I can remember it was you and your partner here who orchestrated this plan that went haywire. Don't put it on me. Oh no! I had nothing to do with this"

Domenico took another puff from his cigarette.

"Sorry doc. You are right. It was our fuck up. Now, what do you propose we do?"

"Bring her in. She is the only contact that Charlie trusts. There is no one else... that will be able to read... Charlie's thoughts. She is his only receiver... no one else. There is nothing stronger in this world... than the bond that exists... between a mother... and her son. Let's bring her in... before anybody else gets hurt. Agree?"

Domenico inhaled again from his smoke. "Ok doc. Agreed. We will bring her in"

"What? Are we going to tell her everything sir?" Darren asked nervously

"We do not have any other choice son. Do you have a better idea?"

Clearly irritated by Domenico's decision and the fact that he had betrayed his best friend's secret Darren said to him "I just don't want to get killed by my best friend, that's all"

"I'll have to make some calls first to obtain a waiver for an interim clearance for Mrs. Winston before we brief her" Domenico explained

"You are making the correct decision... agent Domenico..." doctor Lobowski said as she opened the door to building nine eleven and closed the door behind her.

"Do you want to make the call son?" Domenico asked Darren
"Call? To who?"

"To the Winstons, of course. Who else?"

"Are you serious sir? Why me sir?" Darren asked frightened

"Why you? Because it is part of your job agent Johnson, that's why" Domenico replied to him

"With all due respect sir, I know exactly what my job description and duties are. What it does not say is for me to betray my best friend and his family sir" Darren answered now irritated

Agent Domenico took a few steps and stood close to Darren's face who clearly felt very uncomfortable at his moment.

"Look agent Johnson. As an FBI agent you are going to encounter many uncomfortable, uneasy situations, and sadly, this is one of them. You are going to question many of the orders given to you by your superiors, believe me, I have gone thu that too. But you must control your emotions. Do you understand son?" Domenico tried to explain

Darren put his left palm over his forehead as if checking his body temperature. He then scratched his hair and started pacing around the front entrance of the building for about a minute. He then said to Domenico "Ok, shit! I'm fucked either way if I call them or not" as he started to dial Tom's number on his cell phone. But before he finished dialing his number Domenico interrupted him.

"Darren. Stop." he said to him "don't call them"

"But sir..." Darren answered confused

"Hang up son. I'll do it. I will call them from my cell phone. I said hang up!" he ordered Darren

"Yes sir" Darren said as he complied

Domenico started pacing himself, moving his cell phone from one hand to the other while Darren just stared at him without saying a word. Darren knew it was a very hard thing for him to do as well. And for that, he respected the man. Dolan Domenico finally had the courage and dialed the Winston's number from his cell phone. Tom answered the call.

"Tom...this is agent Dolan Domenico. Tom, I have something to tell you"

11

Darren listened attentively as Dolan Domenico explained to Tom on his phone the strange events that have occured during the past forty eight hours. How the agency had devised a plan to abduct Charlie, the reason behind it, why they have not told him of the plan, and why Lydia was kept in the dark because of security reasons. Tom was silent at the other end of the line, probably in shock, Domenico thought to himself.

"You still there Tom?" Domenico asked

"I'm here sir. I just can't believe what you just told me"

"Do you want me to talk to your wife Tom?"

"You better not sir. She would want to see you castrated"

"I understand. But I can assure you Tom, your son is fine"

"How did you find out about our sessions with doctor Lobowski sir?" Tom asked curiously

"Well…"Domenico started saying, but suddenly Tom interrupted. "Nope. You don't have to tell me sir. There is only one person who I talked to about that. Is he there with you?"

Domenico hesitated at first, then said "yes he is. But you have to understand, the plan was totally my idea Tom. Agent Johnson had nothing to do with it. You got it?"

"Sure…sir" Tom said in a hesitant way "I will let the Fredericksburg Police know that he is safe and sound. No need to get them involved"

After Tom said this Domenico could hear Lydia on the background screaming and asking Tom about Charlie.

"They found Charlie Tom? Where is he? Is he safe? Can we go see him?" Domenico heard Lydia say on the background.

"Sir, I better go. I have some explaining to do to my wife"

"Remember Tom. The Gulfstream jet will be waiting for you both at the airport. Take your time. We will see you both soon" concluded Domenico

"Yes sir" Tom replied

"And Tom, you can do to me whatever you desire. Like I said, it was my idea. I can take it"

"If I was you sir I would not be worried about me. I would be worrying about the reaction from my wife instead" Tom said, and then the line went dead.

"Shit! What a fucking mess!" Domenico whispered

"How did they take it sir?" Darren asked anxiously

"Just as we expected them to take it agent Johnson. I guess I better go shopping for another pair of testicles" said Dolan

Now, it was up to Tom to describe to Lydia the very unusual circumstances of their son disappearance.

"What did the police told you Tom?" Lydia asked anxiously

"Charlie is ok honey, thank God" replied Tom

"Where is he? Can we go see him? Are they bringing him home?" she asked in despair

"No. Not yet honey. Not exactly"

"What do you mean Tom, not yet?"

Tom started rubbing his chin thinking about the precise words to say before starting with the explanation to Lydia.

"What is going on Tom? Is Charlie's kidnapping has something to do with your job, a reprisal from some criminals?" Lydia asked

"No it's not honey"

"Well then? Who was on the phone Tom?"

"Honey, please sit down. I have some explaining to do"

Lydia carefully sat on one of their breakfast nook chairs without taking her eyes off Tom. Tom sat across from her.

"That was not the police on the phone, was it?" Lydia said

Tom slightly moved his head side to side.

"Honey, a few days ago I told Darren about our visits with doctor Lobowski" Tom started saying while he breathed hard. "We were...at the cafeteria...and we just started a conversation over breakfast and, the subject of you and Charlie came up"

"What exactly did you tell him Tom?"

"About the visits to doctor Lobowski, the sessions we had and the strange experiences we all encountered while we were there"

"Why Tom? That is our personal life Tom!" cried out Lydia

"Well, he has been my best and closest friend ever since we were at the academy. I was stressed, and like I said, the conversation just led to Charlie's situation"

"Jesus, Tom! How could you? Lydia cried upset

"Sorry honey. It was not my intention to bring any harm to Charlie babe. I'm so sorry" Tom replied grabbing both of Lydia's hands

"I don't understand Tom. What does all of this has to do with our son Charlie?" Lydia asked him

"It looks like Darren could not contain himself and told agent Domenico all about our chat at the cafeteria"

"So, your boss knows too?"

"Yes honey, he does. And that's where Charlie's disappearance came into play" Tom tried to explain to Lydia

"What? What the hell are you involved in Tom?" Lydia asked angrily

Tom cleared his throat first, the continued as best he could with his explanation of Charlie's abduction. Before he could say anything else Lydia injected

"Did agent Dolan Domenico took our son?"

"No. Not him specifically. Looks like it was a carefully executed plan by the FBI. And masterminded by Dolan Domenico, and Darren"

"What the fuck Tom! Are you telling me that your boss and your so called best friend at the FBI concocted a plan to kidnap Charlie? Is that what you are telling me Tom?" Lydia asked now baffled by all Tom was telling her

"Yes. That's what it looks like Lydia" Tom answered her

"Why? Why in the hell would they do that? For what?"

"Domenico told me that the FBI confiscated all of doctor Lobowski's videos she recorded from our sessions. After they examined them they concluded that...that they needed to examine Charlie's powers farther, with the help of some experts"

Lydia suddenly stood up and removed her hands from under Tom's. She was very, very angry. Angry at the fact that persons she knew could take away her son without her consent, for any reason. She was angry at the fact that a government agency had such powers as to abduct her Charlie without any repercussions.

"What are they doing to him Tom?" What do they want from Charlie? For God's sake, he is only a boy, only thirteen years old!" she screamed

"He is fine honey. Domenico assured me he is ok"

"Domenico assured you, you say? The same fucker that took our son? Do you believe that son of a bitch?" Lydia yelled

"He explained to me it is a matter of national security. He said he will explain further when we get there" Tom replied

"Where? Where is Charlie? When can we see him?"

"They are somewhere in northern Nevada. In a secured location. They already arranged transportation for us to get there. Domenico also is getting things in order to obtain a temporary security clearance for you so he can brief you on the whole plan"

"I don't want any goddamn security clearance Tom! I just want our son back home with us. Do you hear me?" Lydia screamed again

"I hear you honey. I do!"

Lydia grabbed her purse, put her phone and some personal items inside of it and carefully folded Charlie's shirt she had been holding to all of this time. She then turned to Tom and gave him an almost maniacal look.

"Let's go get our boy Tom" she calmly said to Tom

12

The Winstons arrived at building nine eleven seven hours later. After greeting them at the front entrance Miss Helen Machado hurriedly guided them to a room where Domenico and agent Johnson were waiting for them.

"What is this place?" Lydia asked Helen

Helen Machado, the General Manager and caretaker of the secret building located on the middle of the Nevada desert, just glanced at Lydia and gave her a slight smile without saying a word. Lydia followed her clutching Charlie's shirt in front of her chest. They arrived at one of the guest rooms and Helen knock softly on the door.

"Come on in" Dolan's voice was heard behind the door. Dolan Domenico was standing in the middle of the room while Darren Johnson was seated in front of a large square brown table with seven other chairs around it. No one said anything to each other for about ten seconds until Domenico greeted Tom and Lydia. He then extended his right hand to Lydia and said to her "I'm glad…" he started. But before he could finish Lydia had swung her right arm and slapped him hard on his left cheek.

"Where is my son?" she demanded from Domenico "what have you done with my son!" she yelled again to him

Domenico just stood there. He had expected this reaction from her.

"I assure you Mrs. Winston, Charlie is..." he started again. But again he was not able to finish his sentence as Lydia swung this time her left arm and slapped him hard again on his right cheek.

"Do not say his name, you son of a bitch! I want to see my son now!" she again demanded

Domenico could see her diabolical look on her face, just as Tom had warned him earlier on the phone. Lydia was about to swing again and plant another one on Domenico when Tom stepped in

"Lydia, please! Let him talk!" Tom said to her

"No. It's ok son. I deserve it. I can understand the way she feels" Domenico said to Tom

"No you don't Mr. Domenico. You don't have any fucking idea how am I feeling right now. You don't have any idea what we have been thru during the past two days. Have any of your children been kidnapped before by people you know and trust?" Lydia asked

"No Mrs. Winston they have not" Dolan replied bowing his head a little

"Then you don't have any fucking idea how I feel now agent Domenico. Believe me, you don't!" Lydia responded angrily

"Tom, Lydia...can I talk to you both about something important before we go see your son?" Domenico asked them

"No you may not. I want to see Charlie now!" Lydia demanded

"Very well. Fair enough" Domenico replied

Before leaving the room Lydia took a look at Darren who had been quietly watching the whole scene. She turned to him and said "and you, I thought you were my husband's best friend. how could you be part of this evil scheme Darren?"

Darren did not respond to Lydia, and only lowered his head in shame for what he had done to the Winstons.

Dolan Domenico then interrupted and said "Mrs. Winston, he had nothing to do with it. The whole plan was my idea. I assure you both"

"That may well be the case agent Domenico. But he broke my husband's trust by telling you about our personal life after Tom specifically told him to keep it to himself" Lydia explained

A sudden cry came out from Darren's mouth, his head was still down as if he had been reprimanded by his school teacher.

"I'm sorry. I'm so sorry Tom, Lydia. I was selfish. I was only thinking about advancing my career at the agency. Please forgive me!" Darren cried out

Tom looked at the man he considered his best friend. He looked by all means remorseful for what he had done, but he was not about to let him off the hook. At least not yet. Tom then turned to Domenico.

"Sir, I want to make a trade with you"

"Trade? What do you mean trade?" Dolan asked surprised

Tom pulled out his newly issued FBI credentials, his badge, and weapon and laid them on the table in front of Darren.

"I'll trade you all of this for my son sir" Tom indicated

"What? What the hell you mean Tom? You don't need to do this son. There is no need for this. We are going to see your son now"

"I don't want them" Tom started saying "I don't think I can trust the agency or my job at this moment sir"

"Tom, are you willing to throw away your FBI career?"

"Yes sir I would. I would do anything for our son"

Tom and Lydia embraced while Darren and Domenico glanced at each other. Lydia whispered to Tom.

"Are you sure about this honey?" she said to Tom

Tom just nodded his head.

"Ok son. If that's the way you want to play it. Very well then. Please follow me" Dolan instructed Tom and Lydia

They walked thru the narrow hallway until they arrived at the guest room where Charlie and doctor Lobowski were staying. Upon seeing his parents Charlie ran into their arms and they all hugged for a very long time. Lydia checked his face, gave him multiple kisses on his face and then asked him crying loud "are you ok Charlie?"

"Yes mom. Ok" Charlie simply responded

"Oh my god Charlie! We were so worried about you!"
"How are you doing son?" Tom asked him
"Good dad" answered Charlie
"Are you hurt? Did they do anything to you?"
"No. We just played a game" Charlie said to Tom
"Game? What game?" Tom asked curiously
"The game with the doctors before we go to Disney World"
"Game, Disney World? What's all this about Domenico?" Tom asked
Domenico shook his head and then replied "I'll explain later Tom"
"No you don't need to agent Domenico" Lydia began saying "It looks like to me that you bribed a thirteen year old boy with fancy tales of games and a trip to Disney World in order to drag him to this dungeon you guys call a secure location. You really are a piece of work Mr. Domenico. Shame on you!" she concluded

"If you let me explain, Mrs. Winston. You will understand why we took such drastic measures" Domenico said

Lydia was kneeling in front of Charlie when she instantly stood up and started yelling at Domenico

"You fucker...motherfucker, fucker! Who the hell you think you are? You have no right..." she continued screaming to Dolan when she noticed doctor Lobowski's small figure.

"Doctor Lobowski? What are you doing here? Were you part of this also?" Lydia asked her

Tom had been so preoccupied with Charlie that he did not notice the doctor until Lydia called on her.

"Doctor Lobowski?" he asked

Doctor Lobowski slowly approached them.

"Well, hello again Mr. and Mrs. Winston. Sorry that...we have to meet...under these circumstances..."

"Why are you here doc?" Tom asked her

"Well...it was not by choice...believe me..."

"What do you mean doctor Lobowski?" Lydia asked

"It was either...I would cooperate...or agent Domenico here... threaten me with jail...and ruin my career"

Lydia turned to Domenico "Like I said before, you really are a piece of work" she said

"Can we go to Disney World now mom?" Charlie interrupted

"Yes Charlie. But first, we need to go home and pack, ok?"

"Ok mom" Charlie answered

"Mrs. Winston, Tom, will you give me a chance to tell the side of my story now?" asked Domenico

"And why should we do that Mr. Domenico?" asked Lydia

"Well...maybe because we want to prevent another missile crisis and maybe...keep world peace?"

"Oh...really..." Lydia said unfazed by Domenico's remarks

Darren then joined the conversation and said "Mrs. Winston, I know you hate me at this very moment because of what I did, but trust me, agent Domenico went out of his way in order to obtain a special temporary security clearance to brief you on this classified operation"

"What classified operation?" Lydia asked

"Let me clarify Mrs. Winston. What agent Johnson means is that after we found out about your son Charlie we organized a plan to analyze further your son's capabilities. We decided to bring three of the world's most renowned neuroscientists to assist us in studying Charlie's faculties. We also asked doctor Lobowski to join us since Charlie had her trust following your sessions." Domenico explained

""And how did that go?" asked Lydia

"Not too well" doctor Lobowski inserted

"That's when we decided to call upon you both"

"On my request, of course" doctor Lobowski added

"Mr. Domenico, are you treating our son like a guinea pig to study his powers?" asked Lydia

"Absolutely not Mrs. Winston. I can promise you that"

"Well then, what is the purpose of all this. What do you want from us agent Domenico?"

"Can we all sit down please?" Domenico requested

After everyone was seated Domenico continued "as Darren indicated I was able to obtain an interim security clearance for Mrs. Winston to be able to brief her on this. Mrs. Winston, you probably heard the news lately concerning the Russian Navy approaching Ecuadorian waters and the Panama Canal."

"Yes I have. And the mess it has created in California…"

"Well, we have been following very closely the alliance between Russian President Perchenko and his counterpart President Melancón of Ecuador. But, even with all of the latest and greatest technology that we currently have in the world of intelligence nothing is better and more reliable than what we call HUMIT, or human intelligence. Do you understand me, Mrs. Winston?"

"Yes, like a spy" replied Lydia

"That is correct. Although we have been following developments regarding movements with the Russian Navy we really do not know what the Russian President real motives are. We need to know by any means possible what his next move is"

"And, how do you plan to do that?"

"By reading his mind, Mrs. Winston" said Domenico

"And, what does this has to do with our family?"

"Well, specifically you and Charlie, Mrs. Winston. The ability of Charlie's telepathic powers and your receiving abilities will help us achieve this" Dolan explained

"What exactly are you asking my wife and son to do sir?" asked Tom surprised

"I am asking your wife and son to be a part of a classified campaign led by the agency and the CIA Tom"

"What? What campaign is that sir?"

"It's called Operation Carondelet" Domenico indicated to Tom

"Why my family sir? Why put them in jeopardy instead of using assets from the agency and the CIA?"

"We will not be able to get close enough to Perchenko Tom, and you know it. We already tried to connect Charlie with our scientists and obviously it did not go as planned"

"No it didn't. That's for sure" doctor Lobowski said

"Thank you for reminding me doctor" Domenico replied annoyed by her remarks

"And how exactly are you planning to get close to Perchenko sir. Do you want us to go knocking at his office at the Kremlin?" Tom asked sarcastically

"Of course not Tom. But, we expect President Melancón to have a Presidential inauguration gala soon. And we are sure Perchenko will be there to show his support"

"Let me guess. At Carondelet Palace"

"You got it son" Domenico replied

"So, let me get this straight. You want my wife Lydia and my only son Charlie to attend this gala at Carondelet Palace in Quito, Ecuador, get close enough to Russian President Perchenko, and to try to read his mind? And hopefully, we can then learn what these two nuts are up to next? Did I miss anything sir?" Tom asked

"Actually, yes. If they decide to go with this Mrs. Winston will have to...will have to... let's say, wear a revealing dress, low cut, with plenty of cleavage. Perchenko likes women with let's say...big assets?" Domenico explained and then cleared his throat

"No fucking way Tom. I will not put our son in danger. This is madness!" Lydia yelled

"I agree sir. This is too risky for my family"

"You kidnapped our son, used him as a guinea pig, and now you are asking us to go to a foreign country, and get involved in some illegal activity there involving corrupt world politicians. You have some nerve Domenico. You are out of your fucking mind!" Lydia responded at the same time she covered both of Charlie's ears. She then whispered to Domenico "what else you want me to do? Suck Perchenko's dick?" she asked. Lobowski chuckled after hearing Lydia.

"No Mrs. Winston. I am sure it will not have to come to that"

"What is going to be her cover? I'm sure they will be suspicious of anyone new there" asked Tom

"We already took care of that. We briefed ambassador Calvares and he will introduce her as his new assistant and her son from the United States"

"Don't know sir. It still sounds too risky to me sir"

"All of our assets will be in place there Tom. If anything goes wrong they will be extracted immediately and flown back home to the states. I guarantee you that. You have my word" Domenico assured Tom

"Well, it's not up to me. All of this sounds crazy but it will be up to Lydia and Charlie" Tom said "What do you think honey?"

"I think it's not up to me and Charlie to fight other countries wars. That's what I think Tom" replied Lydia

Dolan Domenico knew that time was of the essence, and that a conflict could happen at any time. He decided to take it upon himself to try to convince Lydia. He turned to her and looked straight into her eyes.

"Listen Mrs. Winston. I understand why you are reluctant about this whole plan. We were hoping that we would learn enough from Charlie so none of you would need to get personally involved. But that turned out not to be the case. As doctor Lobowski said, you are the only connection that Charlie trusts, the only person on this planet that he will transmit his thoughts to, *you*, are his only receiver. I know right now you despise me, along with, some of my colleagues here. But I ask you not to do this for me or them, but for the sake of our country. For the sake of our children's future. For the sake of a better world. Let me put it bluntly, Mrs. Winston. You and Charlie may be the last hope we all have at preventing a possible nuclear encounter with the Russian Federation. That's all I have to say" Domenico concluded as he stood up. He then added "I hope for god's sake that you will think about it. But, not for long, as time is not on our side Mrs. Winston. Have a good flight back home" he said as he turned away from Lydia and left the room.

Tom, Lydia and their son Charlie were on their way home to Virginia on the Gulfstream jet provided by the agency. Tom and Lydia were ecstatic to have their son back. Not much was said during the first half hour of the flight. Tom was catching up on his sleep after going thru so much during the past couple of days. Lydia held Charlie close to her on the aisle next to his.

"Tom, Tom, Tom?" Lydia tried to wake him up

"What honey? Are we home yet? Is Charlie ok?" Tom asked startled

"Charlie is ok hun. He is sleeping" Lydia responded

"Lucky him. Ooooops...here we go..." he said as he brought his seat back straight up "what is going on honey?"

"Do you think I should do it?"

"Do what Lydia?"

"The plan. The secret operation stuff your boss talked about. The caron thing..." Lydia said

"Oh. You mean the Carondelet Operation"

"Yes, that. Do you think me and Charlie should do it?"

Tom grabbed Lydia's hand before saying to her "Like I told him honey, it's up to you and Charlie"

"What would you do if you were on my shoes?" asked Lydia

"Well, if I were you babe I would do what would be best for Charlie's future. For anyone's future" Tom answered

"Why do we have to be the ones with that heavy responsibility on our shoulders? The ones to save the world? Why us?"

"Maybe because... that's what god's plan was for Charlie and you. For you both to have that special bond, that special connection. For a better and brighter future for our son honey" Tom said as he squeezed Lydia's hand.

Just then, Lydia's mobile phone rang. Lydia recognized the number right away as the number from Boston Memorial Hospital, where her sister Lily had been admitted.

"What is going on Lydia?" Tom asked her concerned as Lydia's eyes started to tear up after answering the call.

"It's Lily Tom! She is gone! Oh my god Tom! She is gone!" Lydia cried out

At once, Tom jumped from his seat and walked into the cockpit.

He pleaded to the captain of the Gulfstream jet "Can we detour to Boston Logan International please? It's an emergency!"

"Sure sir. What is the emergency sir?" the captain asked

"It's my wife's sister. She just passed away" Tom replied

The service was simple, between family and close friends, just as Lily had requested. Her body was cremated and laid to rest next to her mother's grave. The family and close friends gathered at Lydia's home where they shared stories and glanced at family pictures while Tom tried to comfort Lydia and her family in this time of great sadness. Tom was coming out of the kitchen with more appetizers when Lydia grabbed him by the arm.

"Thank you honey. Everyone loved the food" she said to Tom

"You are all welcome dear" Tom replied and gave her a light kiss on her forehead

"By the way Tom, where is Charlie?" asked Lydia

"I thought he was outside playing with his cousins"

"Don't worry, I will check on him. Thanks again"

Lydia grabbed a few of the appetizers from the tray on the kitchen counter and put some on a small, disposable plate. She then looked around for Charlie. She went outside but did not see him, and decided to walk upstairs to his room. She approached his room's door but it was unusually quiet. No music was playing, no UFC bouts blasting from his television. To her surprise Charlie was inside his room quietly drawing on his desk. Lydia silently approached him and placed the plate with appetizers on his bed.

"Hello Charlie. What are you doing honey?" she asked him

"I'm drawing" Charlie responded

"Drawing what honey?"

"A picture"

"A picture. What type of picture?" curiously asked Lydia

"A picture of me, dad, you and aunt Lily"

"Really. Can I see it? Here, I brought you some of the cheese crackers with tuna you like. You hungry?"

"Yes" Charlie answered as he reached for the plate and sat on his bed. Lydia looked at the pictures Charlie had just completed.

"Is this me honey?" Lydia asked him pointing to one of the figures on Charlie's drawing.

"Yes mom. And this is dad, and this is me" Charlie replied pointing at the two other figures.

"And who is this... lady on top of a cloud?"

"That is auntie Lily" Charlie replied "she is flying to heaven"

Lydia's eyes started to get red and tears started to wet his cheeks

"Mom, is auntie Lily on heaven now?" Charlie inquired

"Yes she is Charlie" Lydia replied trying to hold her tears

"Will we see her when we go to heaven too?"

"Sure we will honey. We will see all of our family that is now in heaven. Aunt Lily, grandma and grandpa"

"I heard aunt Lily again mom" Charlie said to Lydia

"When Charlie? When did you heard from her?"

"When I was sleeping on the plane"

"You mean when we were coming back home on the nice plane?"

"Yes" Charlie answered. Lydia sat next to him on his bed while he started to eat one of the cheese crackers and tuna. She wanted to hear more from Charlie.

"Charlie, honey. What exactly did you hear from auntie Lily?"

"That she was sad that she could not stay with us, and that she loved me, you, and dad lots. And that she needed to go to heaven so she could rest. She said she was very tired"

Lydia wiped her tears with her left hand and started sobbing, trying to restrain herself in front of her son.

"And, what else did you hear Charlie?"

"Auntie Lily said that all of us should always love each other and do what is best for our friends, and our families. And she said that all of us always get a chance in life to do great things, to make the world better. And that we must act on that chance" Charlie explained to Lydia

"I am so proud of you Charlie. Listen to you. You sound so mature already" Lydia told Charlie as she fixed his hair

"I was only listening to what auntie Lily said mom"

"I know you were honey. I know you were" Lydia responded and gave him a kiss on his head. Then she added "thank you Charlie, for letting me recognize *that chance* honey"

"You are welcome" Charlie said

"Do you want to come downstairs and play with your cousins?"

"No mom. I want to draw some more"

"Sure. Go ahead honey. I'll see you later downstairs, ok?"

"Ok mom" Charlie answered her. He then finished eating the last snack, sat back on his desk, and started drawing again.

Lydia glanced at Charlie for a few seconds, and then left his room quietly. Most of the close friends already had left and some of her relatives were chatting among each other in the family room continuing to share short stories about Lily. Her accomplishments, commitment to causes, and her desire to help people in need, especially those stricken with cancer. Lydia stepped into the kitchen where Tom had his back to her preparing more appetizers on the kitchen counter. He did not notice her until she embraced him around his waist.

"Thank you for being a great partner Tom" Lydia said

Tom turned around and noticed Lydia's tears on her face. He handled her some tissues.

"I know it's been hard for you. But we are all here to support you" Tom said to her

Lydia wiped her tears and then said "I'll do it"

"Do what honey?"

"The operation…"

"What? Operation?" Tom asked her shaking his head

"With Mr. Domenico. Agent Domenico's plan with me and Charlie" Lydia responded

"Oh… honey. This is not the time for us to discuss that"

"No, it's fine. I'm fine, Charlie is fine. I'm ok with it"

"Lydia, I still feel is not safe for you and Charlie to get involved in Operation Carondelet" Tom tried to convince Lydia

"Do you trust the agency, your boss, your colleagues?" asked Lydia

"Of course I do Lydia. I'm still pissed at them, but by all means I trust them. Yes" Tom answered

"With your life?"

"Yes, I would honey"

"Well then? I will trust them with mine and Charlie's"

Startled by Lydia's sudden change of attitude he asked her "what made you change your mind Lydia? Was it Domenico's last words before we left building nine eleven?"

"That was part of it, yes. But mainly it was the last words from my sister Lily to Charlie. I loved her so much!" said Lydia

"Well, I understand honey. If you and Charlie are up to it I will call Domenico tomorrow and let him know that we can proceed with Operation Carondelet"

"Please do. Let's do this" Lydia said proudly

"But for now, you can help me with all of these dishes"

"You wash, I'll dry" Lydia replied

13

Erin Burnett was reporting the breaking news on CNN.

"We now have our Pentagon correspondent Barbara Starr standing by the defense department waiting for defense secretary Donovan's briefing, at which time, we will go there live. Barbara, can you give us a preview of what secretary Donovan is going to talk about?" she asked

"Yes Erin. We expect the secretary to address the tensions between the United States and Russia, as the Russian Navy fleet gets closer and closer to Ecuadorian waters. Although Russian President Perchenko has indicated many times that the Russian ships are going there at the request of Ecuadorian President Melancón the White House continues to question what are the real intentions of President Perchenko and the constant rumors of possibly bringing mobile ballistic nuclear missiles to the Galapagos Archipelago. Neither the White House or the President, are happy about this. Erin?"

"And, Barbara, as you stated there is speculation of possible installations of these missiles on these islands that belong to the country of Ecuador. And these are just a few thousand miles from the western United States" Erin Burnett responded

"That is correct Erin. These small islands are actually less than three thousand miles from the city of Los Angeles and for this reason you can imagine the tension it has created between the two nuclear superpowers as these ships inch closer to the waters of Ecuador. This indeed has created tensions not seen since the Cuban Missile crisis in the sixties during the Kennedy administration" Barbara Starr reported

"Yes. And as a matter of fact Barbara, it has already created panic especially in California where it has been reported that residents there have purchased thousands of weapons and ammunition after rumors spread on social media of an imminent Russian invasion thru the west coast"

"Yes it has Erin. But according to the White House the President has been in close contact with the governor of California and assured him of complete support from the administration concerning the protection and safety of all Californians. Erin, back to you" Barbara concluded

Erin Burnett was about to respond when secretary Donovan entered the briefing room. He walked to the podium with a thin folder on his right hand. Erin interrupted the reporting exchange between her and Barbara Starr.

"Ok, we are now going live to the defense department where secretary Donovan is about to give his briefing. Let's listen"

Defense secretary Donovan stood by the podium and took a sip of water before starting in a room packed with reporters.

"Good afternoon ladies and gentlemen" he started saying as multiple flashes from cameras flooded the media room. He then continued.

"This will be a short briefing and I will not take any questions after. Ladies and gentlemen, members of the press, and the American people, as you are all aware by now, the defense department has been monitoring the movement of the Russian Federation's forty third missile ship division since it left Severomorsk, Russia. Russian President Nikolai Perchenko has made assurances that the Russian fleet is traveling to Ecuadorian waters at the request of President Eduardo Amador Melancón for joint exercises with the Ecuadorian

Navy. But, the White House is concerned that the Russian Navy fleet may be carrying multiple nuclear warhead missiles with a range capable of reaching the western United States. These missiles could, and I say again, could, be possibly be based on the Galapagos Archipelago, less than three thousand miles from the California coast. Our President has been in constant communication with President Perchenko and expressed the concern from the administration regarding this volatile situation. The President's administration wants to make it very clear to Russian President Perchenko and the Russian people. We do not want any type of conflict with the Russian Federation. But at the same time, we will protect any South or Central American nation that would feel threatened by the Russian ships, especially the country of Panama, who already has contacted us with their concern for the safety of the Panama Canal. I emphasize again, our President wants to make it clear that although both, Presidents Perchenko and Melancón have stated that their purpose is peaceful military exercises between the two countries, the United States military will be ready to defend any of our allies in Central and South America and vows to protect the Panama Canal, the most important maritime trade business conduit in the world. The President continues to monitor the situation closely and also continues talks with the Russian President regarding this tense affairs. This is all we have for now. Thank you all for coming and god bless the United States of America" secretary Donovan concluded with his briefing. Secretary Donovan then walked away from the podium among a blast of questions from the reporters without answering any of them. The CNN cameras came back to Erin Burnett who asked Barbara Starr "Barbara, what did you get from secretary Donovan's briefing?"

"Well Erin, it looks like the President and the defense department are really concerned where all of this may end up. Like he said towards the end, the United States military is ready, and vows, to protect our Latin American allies from any possible aggression from the

Russian Navy and especially Erin, the Panama Canal, which is the largest transit for business traffic in the world" Barbara replied

"Any comments from the White House after the secretary's briefing?" Erin asked

"No, no comment at all. But we were able to get reaction from a defense department official after we asked if the United States was ready to use military force if the Panama Canal was blocked by the Russian Navy. This spokesperson said Erin, quote, 'that is not going to happen. I guarantee you that' unquote. Erin, back to you" Barbara closed on her reporting

Dolan Domenico was attentively listening to the breaking news in his office when Tom knocked on his door. He turned off the power to the television.

"Come in Tom" he yelled

Tom, Lydia and Charlie then stepped into his office.

"What a great surprise. I am very glad the whole family is here. Mrs. Winston, are you one hundred percent sure you want to proceed with this?" he asked Lydia

"Yes I am" Lydia replied

"What made you change your mind Mrs. Winston?"

"Please call me Lydia"

"Ok Lydia. Why the change now? You were pretty upset the last time we spoke" Dolan stated

"I know I was. But after my sister's death… and, what you said to me in Nevada, and after words from Charlie, I decided that it *is* the right thing to do" Lydia answered

"I'm really sorry about your sister Lydia. My deepest condolences. Tom told me on the phone"

"Thank you Mr. Domenico. I appreciate that. Although we were expecting it, it doesn't make it any easier. It still hard to process still"

"Please call me Dolan" Domenico said

"Ok Dolan. So, what next? Do I get to drive an Aston Martin like double oh seven?" Lydia asked jokingly

"I'm afraid not. I will introduce you to the team and brief you and Tom. I will let you talk to Charlie and explain the best way you decide"

"Are we going to Disney World mom?" Charlie asked

"No honey. Not this time. But, we are going to go to an exotic country called Ecuador. What do you think about that Charlie?" Lydia asked him

"Do they have castles there like Disney World?"

"Not exactly honey. But we get to visit a real castle. A big castle called Carondelet. Isn't that great?"

Charlie's eyes opened wide and surprised he asked Lydia "really mom? A real castle?"

"Yes we are Charlie. We will be leaving soon"

"When mom? When are we going to see the castle mom?" Charlie asked excited now

"Soon honey. Very soon. Me and dad need to talk to some people to make the arrangements, then we will be on our way there" Lydia promised Charlie

"Yay mom! I can't wait!" exclaimed Charlie

While Lydia and Charlie were chatting Dolan had been talking on his phone. He said to the person at the other end of the line "Yes, they are here. Come in to my office" and then hung up.

Dolan turned to Lydia and Tom "before we go into the briefing room someone wants to see you both" he said

"Really? Who?" asked Tom

There was a soft knock on Domenico's office door and Darren Johnson entered. He was trying hard to hide something behind his back as he slowly approached Tom and Lydia. He was a little nervous as he started to address them.

"Tom, Lydia, Charlie. I sincerely apologize for breaking the family trust you gave to me. Tom, you are like a brother to me and you were the only person that helped me get thru the academy training without me going insane. And here we are. I really hope that this does not affect our friendship, not only with you, but with your family as well. Here... "Darren continued as he brought his hands from behind his back and showed Tom his FBI badge, credentials, and his nine millimeter Glock weapon. "I think you will be needing these when you go to Ecuador" he told Tom. Tom looked at Domenico who just shrugged his shoulders, and then at Lydia, who was standing with her arms crossed in front of her chest. Tom took a long breath, then cleared his throat.

"I believe you Darren. I don't want this to interfere with our friendship either. Next time, keep it between us, ok? Unless I tell you otherwise" Tom replied to Darren.

"You have my word Tom. I swear" Darren said raising his right hand

"You better!" Lydia interrupted "because if it happens again Darren, I will, cut your balls off. Got it?"

"Got it Mrs. Winston. You have my word too!" Darren assured her

"Give me that" Tom said as he grabbed his weapon, credentials, and his FBI badge from Darren and they both hugged.

"Ok, ok... enough male bonding now..."Domenico started saying "Darren, please stay here in my office with Charlie while we attend the briefing in room 303A" he instructed Darren

"Yes sir" replied Darren

"And Lydia" Dolan said looking at her "one of our female officers will be showing you a dress to wear for the gala, with your approval, and Tom's, of course"

"Oh my!... Lydia started jokingly "do you hear that Tom? I get to wear a sexy dress and show my tits to the Russian President! Isn't that exciting honey?" she asked Tom

Tom pretended to ignore Lydia and instead turned to Dolan and said to him "I think you just created a monster sir"

"Hum... I guess I have agent Winston, I guess I have" Dolan replied as they all left his office towards room 303A

14

Presidential Inauguration Gala
Carondelet Presidential Palace, Quito, Ecuador

*P*alacio de Carondelet [Carondelet Palace] is a majestic structure located in the heart of the city of Quito, Ecuador. It was indeed an impressive site for Tom, Lydia, and Charlie who all admired the many marble columns and detailed arches of the palace that was named after Francisco Luis Héctor de Carondelet, a well known Ecuadorian political figure during the late eighteen hundreds. The inaugural presidential gala was to be held at the Presidential Hall or what some called the Yellow Room, because of the yellow wallpaper decorating the room. The Yellow Room was accessorized with the pictures of all Ecuador's Presidents along the top of the walls and the ceiling was adorned in unique hexagon shapes carved in wood. The Winston family had been admiring the city sights having arrived there days before the expected Presidential gala and awaiting word of President Perchenko's arrival. The call was finally received and Tom picked up the secured satellite mobile phone. Tom answered it but did not say anything waiting for instructions. He recognized the voice on the line right away as that of Dolan Domenico.

"According to our sources Perchenko will be arriving at Carondelet Palace in approximately two hours" Domenico said

"Got it sir" Tom responded "they will be ready" he added glancing at Lydia

"Great news. Our team will be in place and ready for any situation. Your family is in good hands, agent Winston"

"Thank you sir. That's good to know"

"Will see you inside our mobile unit then" Domenico replied and then the line went dead

"Are you ready honey?" Tom asked Lydia

"Almost Tom" Lydia answered

About ten minutes later Lydia emerged from the bathroom. She was wearing a black evening dress tight to her body, with low cleavage. She was wearing a thin gold necklace with a heart pendant at the end, and gold heart shaped earrings that complemented her necklace. Tom stood in front of her, she took his breath away.

"Well, what do you think hun?" Lydia asked him raising her arms and turning around to show Tom

"You look stunning Lydia!" Tom exclaimed staring at her

"Thank you honey. Let's see if the Russian President will notice"

"I know he will babe. He will be charmed by your beauty"

"Thank you honey. You are so sweet" Lydia answered him

"The ambassador's private vehicle will be here in around twelve minutes. Are you both ready?"

"Yes we are. Come on Charlie" Lydia called on him

Charlie was wearing dress pants with black shoes, a light blue long sleeve shirt, and a red tie.

"Charlie, honey. Are you ready to see the inside of the palace?" Lydia asked him

"Yes" replied Charlie

"Ok guys. Ambassador Calvares will be taking you both to Carondelet Palace. Lydia, once you are inside the palace we will make contact with you and check our communications right away. If anything at all does not feel right to you, or you suspect something wrong let us know ASAP. Other than that, try to relax, and have fun. Or at least, pretend you are" Tom instructed

MEETING AT CARONDELET

"I understand. I will try my best Tom" Lydia replied and then gave Tom a kiss before they all exited the hotel room towards the elevators.

Lydia looked radiant as she entered the Presidential Hall inside Carondelet Palace clutching Charlie's hand. Her heart was pounding as she entered the Yellow Room and dignitaries from all over the world greeted her and ambassador Calvares. They were greeted by the Prime Minister of Perú when she heard a voice on her earpiece.

"You ok Mrs. Winston?" Domenico asked her

"Yes my dear. Doing just fine" Lydia murmured barely moving her lips

Dolan Domenico was communicating with Lydia from a van that was camouflaged as a Univision television affiliate, cleverly parked along the many other news mobile centers.

"Just relax Lydia, and follow ambassador's Calvares lead ok?" Dolan instructed. Lydia did not answer as she shook the hand of another political leader after ambassador Calvares introduced her as his new assistant with her son from the United States.

After five more minutes Tom's voice came on the line.

"You are doing great honey. Perchenko should be there anytime now" Tom said thru her hidden earpiece

Ambassador Calvares then leaned on Lydia's ear "Mrs. Winston, our contact is at three o'clock" he whispered to her

Lydia just nodded in agreement and then turned her head ninety degrees to her right. She recognized Russian President Perchenko dressed in his usual Armani suit, with a glass on his right hand and surrounded by a security detail of eight men. Ambassador Calvares slowly approached him and Lydia's heart pounded even harder. Calvares finally reached Perchenko and extended his hand to him.

"Good evening President Perchenko" he greeted him

"Good evening Mr. ambassador. Nice to see you again" replied Perchenko

"I am glad you could visit Carondelet Palace for such an important event"

"I would not miss it for the world"

"Mr. President, may I introduce you to my new assistant Sara Keeffer and her son Charlie" Calvares said

"Well, it is a pleasure to meet you Miss Keeffer. And hello to you young man" Perchenko said staring at Lydia. He shook Lydia's hand with a strong grip.

"It is an honor to meet you Mister President" Lydia responded

"May I ask where are you from Miss Keeffer?"

"It's... Misses, not Miss. I am married, Mister President" Lydia corrected him

"Oh... pardon me Mrs. Keeffer" Perchenko replied still staring at her

"Good girl" Tom whispered to Lydia on her earpiece

"I am from Virginia sir"

"No need to call me sir Mrs. Keeffer. My friends call me Niko, for Nikolai"

"I'll have to get used to that Mr. President" Lydia said with a soft smile

"What made you take this position here in Ecuador Mrs. Keeffer?" asked Perchenko

"Well... the opportunity to travel with my son, show him different cultures, and earn good money" Lydia answered

Perchenko chuckled and said "of course, of course. And, may I ask, where did you study?" inquired Perchenko

Lydia took a quick glance at ambassador Calvares before answering Perchenko.

"I studied International Politics and Journalism at the University of Washington" she answered him

"Hum... interesting" replied Perchenko

"Sorry to interrupt President Perchenko" ambassador Calvares started "I must introduce my new, beautiful assistant to the other diplomats here" he ended saying

"Sure ambassador Calvares, by all means, you must" replied Perchenko holding his glass of vodka and ice.

"Again, it was my pleasure to meet you Mrs. Keeffer" Perchenko said to Lydia shaking her hand firmly again.

"The pleasure was all mine Mister President" replied Lydia

Ambassador Calvares continued introducing Lydia as his assistant to other dignitaries inside the Presidential Hall. Afterwards, Lydia decided to get a drink for her and Charlie and sat at a table that was reserved for Ambassador Calvares. The ambassador sat next to her.

"Mrs. Winston, I will leave the table in a few seconds. I am going to greet a few friends here. You can then proceed at your own discretion towards your contact. Understood?" he said to Lydia

"I understand Ambassador" Lydia replied

Ambassador Calvares slowly got up from his table and as instructed proceeded to talk with some of his colleagues at the gala. Lydia kept and eye on Perchenko from far away. He was still surrounded by his security detail and was now speaking with Ecuadorian President Melancón, still holding to his glass of vodka and ice. She turned to Charlie.

"Are you having a good time honey?" she asked

"Yes mom. I am having a good time" he answered

"This is a beautiful palace, isn't it?"

"Yes mom. I like this palace."

Lydia then got closer to him and said "Charlie, remember what we talked about earlier at the hotel?"

"Yes mom"

"I want you to really concentrate Charlie, and *listen* really good to what this person says to you. Do you understand Charlie?"

"Yes mom"

Lydia cleared her throat, stood up, and extended her hand to Charlie.

"Are you ready Charlie?"

Charlie did not say anything back. He only nodded his head. They both walked slowly side by side, closer and closer towards Perchenko's entourage. Lydia's heartbeat started to accelerate again, her hand sweaty as she clutched Charlie's hand. She took deep breaths as they inched closer to Perchenko. All of a sudden she heard Domenico's voice again on her earpiece.

"Everything ok Mrs. Winston?" Domenico asked

"Yes. We are approaching him now" Lydia whispered back

"Whenever you are ready Mrs. Winston. We are ready to record"

"Take your time honey" Tom added

Lydia and Charlie continued getting closer towards Perchenko and they both suddenly stopped about thirty feet in front of him. Lydia slowly pulled Charlie in front of her. She then put both of her hands on Charlie's shoulders and slightly squeezed them. She then waited for Charlie to *listen*. It did not take long for Perchenko to notice her presence again. He looked straight at her and raised his glass to acknowledge her. Neither did President Melancón, as he seemed to undress Lydia with his eyes. Lydia started feeling strange again as many times before. She squeezed Charlie's shoulders a little harder. She felt calmness, and a relaxing feeling came upon her. But this time she was not about to faint, because she could control herself, as doctor Lobowski had told her to do. She knew now that whatever was happening it was a very special bond between her and her son. She let Charlie simply *listen* and let him transfer his thoughts to her. And, as it had happened on many previous occasions Lydia started to speak words in a language she never knew, this time in Russian. She was in a complete trance again receiving Charlie's thoughts as Charlie stared stoically at Russian President Perchenko. Lydia was talking in Russian, low enough not to be perceived by others inside the Yellow Room, but loud enough for Domenico's team to record at their mobile unit.

'*Mister Calvares, you sure know how to pick them. She is gorgeous! I wonder if he is fucking her yet?*' Lydia started saying in Russian.

"Did you hear that sir?" Tom asked Domenico

"Yes I did son. Be quiet!..."Domenico whispered back

Lydia continued talking in Russian '*you Americans, you all think you are better and superior to us, you are so conceited and vain. Hah! I wonder how much Miss Keeffer would charge for a night with me? Well... it won't be long Miss Keeffer. Your President is so preoccupied with my ships at the coast of Ecuador that your American friends and families will not know what hit them. You all will be in complete darkness! You sure look fine Miss Keeffer'* Lydia concluded saying in Russian.

"Did you guys got all that?" Domenico asked

"Yes sir. We did. Translation coming soon" a woman behind him said

Inside the Yellow Room one of Perchenko's men noticed something unusual as he looked over at Lydia. He stared at her for a minute and then turned to another man in the security detail.

"That woman, behind the kid with the blue shirt, looks like she was talking to herself, or to someone else" he said

"Go check her out" the other man demanded

"Yes sir" he replied in Russian as he started to walk towards Lydia and Charlie. As he approached, Lydia's trance was interrupted by a loud squeal inside her hidden earpiece. Her eyes opened wide and her head bend down as the high pitch noise got even stronger. She looked forward again towards Perchenko but this time she noticed a tall, muscular Russian man walking towards her and Charlie. She quickly grabbed Charlie's hand and turned around as the bodyguard followed her closely. As he got closer to Lydia and Charlie his earpiece also produced a strong squeal making him suddenly stop. His electronic scanner has been successful in detecting Lydia's earpiece frequency. As Lydia walked away from him he noticed her fumbling with something inside one of her ears. After the squeal had gone away Perchenko's man communicated to his superior.

"She is wired sir. I scanned and detected her earpiece frequency. She was talking to someone sir" he told him

"I believe that is the American Ambassador's new assistant. Miss Keeffer. Go after them and bring them here!" the security chief demanded

Lydia was walking fast towards the front entrance of Carondelet Palace holding Charlie's hand tightly.

"Come on Charlie, we have to go now!" she implored him

She was sweating, her palms were wet, her heart pounding so hard she thought she was having a heart attack. She turned in a hallway with tall marble columns that led to a set of long marble steps. She glanced back nervously and heard the Russian bodyguard steps getting closer to them.

"Lydia, where are you?" Tom asked her

"I am heading towards the grand entrance Tom. One of Perchenko's men is following us. I am scared Tom!" Lydia exclaimed

"Just keep heading towards the grand steps Lydia!" Tom replied

Lydia then heard Domenico's voice on the background as Tom's mike was open "her cover has been compromised. Get them out of there now!" she heard him say

Lydia was now running along with Charlie towards the great marble steps of Carondelet Palace. She quickly glanced again and saw the Russian man getting closer.

"Come on Charlie, run!" she yelled at him

They finally arrived in front of the long marble steps that led to the main entrance at Carondelet Palace. Out of nowhere a woman grabbed Lydia's right arm as she was about to go down the great steps.

"Take your shoes off!" she screamed at Lydia

"What? Who are you?" Lydia asked startled at her sudden appearance

"Don't worry. I'm part of your team Mrs. Winston" she said to Lydia grabbing Charlie and quickly starting down the long steps.

"It will be much easier without your high heels Mrs. Winston. Come on, we don't have too much time!"

Lydia quickly complied and they all started rapidly down the steps. Ambassador Calvares vehicle suddenly appeared at the bottom of the steps waiting for them. When they were half way thru the long marble steps the tall Russian bodyguard appeared on top. He screamed at them in broken English.

"Stop! Misses Keeffer, we need to talk to you!" he yelled

"No you are not Mrs. Winston. Over my dead body. Let's go, hurry!" the unidentified woman said to Lydia

The Russian was now halfway the great steps when Lydia, Charlie and the unknown woman reached the bottom. All three quickly went inside the ambassador's car. As the ambassador's vehicle sped away Perchenko's bodyguard yelled again "Stop, stop, you must stop now!"

"Oh my god, oh my god. Thank you so much! I was so scared. I thought they were going to arrest me and my son. Thanks again!" Lydia said to the woman

"Just doing my job ma'am "she responded

"I lost them sir" the Russian started "they left on the American ambassador's vehicle"

"Come back inside the Presidential Hall. We must find out what they were up to" his superior instructed him

Back inside the Yellow Room Perchenko's chief of security leaned and whispered on his ear what had just happened.

"Do you know this woman President Melancón? This...Miss Keeffer?" Perchenko asked curiously

"No Mister President. This is the first time. Ambassador Calvares just introduced her to me today. Why? Anything wrong?"

"Well, maybe we should ask ambassador Calvares that" replied Perchenko

Calvares was finishing chatting with one of his friends at the gala when he noticed President Melancón waving to him to come over. He approached both of them.

"Good evening President Melancón. Glad to see you again sir. And again, on behalf of the United States we offer you our congratulations on your successful election"

"Thank you ambassador Calvares. President Perchenko here, had some concerns about your new assistant, Miss Keeffer?"

"Sure sir. What seems to be the concern President Perchenko?" Calvares asked playing ignorant

"Well ambassador, it seems like your new assistant left in quite a hurry sir" Perchenko said

"Oh...yes. My driver just called me. He stated that Miss Keeffer was not feeling well so he took her and her son to her apartment"

"Is that so? Too much to drink, perhaps?" asked Perchenko

"No. I think this was too much for her and her young son. Meeting all these strangers and very important people. You know...it can be quite overwhelming" replied Calvares

"Is that her real name ambassador?" asked Perchenko

"What do you mean sir? Of course that is her real name. Miss Sara Keeffer"

"One of my men just happened to detect a communication device that she was wearing at the gala ambassador"

"That is not possible President Perchenko. It must have been an error from his detection equipment" Calvares tried to assure Perchenko.

"Is that what you think Mister ambassador? What if I told you that same man followed her and her son all the way to the main entrance of Carondelet Palace until they got inside your vehicle with another woman. How do you explain that ambassador Calvares?" Perchenko explained

"I would say that he was mistaken. As I said, Miss Keeffer was feeling ill and decided to leave early. That's all"

"Hum..."

"But, if it makes you feel better Mister President, I will check with her and get to the bottom of this. I assure you"

Perchenko got closer to ambassador Calvares until he was just inches from his face "I'm sure you will ambassador" and then took a sip of his vodka and ice. Calvares cleared his throat and replied to Perchenko.

"Well, I have other dignitaries here to greet gentlemen. If you both excuse me. You both enjoy this evening" Calvares concluded and walked away from them. As he walked away he whispered to himself "asshole!"

"What is going on President Perchenko?" inquired Melancón

"I think his so called new assistant is not what she portrayed to be, my friend" said Perchenko

"Do you mean, she is a spy, CIA?"

"Don't really know yet. But I would love to talk to her. She left in a hurry, according to my chief of security"

"Where do you think she left to? To her apartment, as the ambassador said?"

"I don't believe any fucking word from ambassador Calvares. I think she and her son are trying to leave Ecuador as soon as possible" Perchenko speculated

"But why?" Melancón asked

"Why? Because she is hiding something Mister President, that's why!" Perchenko answered raising his voice. He took another sip of his drink and said to Melancón "I want you to do something for me mister President"

"Sure. What do you need?"

"I want you to stop all outgoing flights out of Quito International Airport immediately" Perchenko requested

"But, Mister President. Isn't that a little over…"

"Do it! Now! You, are the elected President of Ecuador, aren't you?" Perchenko asked pointing the finger at Melancón

"Yes sir I am. I will give the order to stop all outgoing flights as a national security measure" Melancón replied

"And thanks for the cheap vodka mister President" Perchenko answered back taking his last sip

Perchenko then proceeded to walk away from the Presidential Hall with his security entourage close to him. As Perchenko exited the Yellow Room Melancón said to himself "fucking Russians!"

"Goliev?" Perchenko asked his chief of security as they walked towards his limousine

"Yes sir?"

"I want you to check if there are any non-commercial aircrafts at Quito Airport right now, especially U.S. military planes. I do not think Miss Keeffer and her son are leaving the country in a commercial flight. Understand?"

"Yes sir" his security chief quickly replied

Seven minutes after traveling on his Presidential limousine Perchenko received a call from Goliev.

"Sir," Goliev started saying "Quito airport reports that a transport C-17 Globemaster cargo plane from the United States Air Force landed here three days ago. Supposedly they were providing humanitarian aid supplies to the Ecuadorian government"

"Humanitarian aid my ass!" said Perchenko angrily "that is their flight out! Call President Melancón and tell him that I said that we need to stop that airplane from taking off Quito International. Is that clear Goliev?"

"Yes sir, right away sir. I will relay your message sir"

"Where are we heading?" Lydia asked nervously

"I was given specific instructions to take you both to Quito airport Mrs. Winston" the ambassador's driver said

"Where is my husband? Is he ok?"

"Agent Winston and the rest of the team are fine Mrs. Winston. No need to worry. They are waiting for us" the unidentified woman said to Lydia

"Thank god!" Lydia said

As they arrived close to Quito airport the woman gave directions to the ambassador's driver.

"Pass the main entrance and continue until the end of the road. Then take a left in front of hangar five" she directed

As they got closer to their destination Lydia could distinguish the shape of the huge C-17 cargo plane with the distinctive United States Air Force markings. The giant back loading ramp was wide open waiting for their precious cargo. Ambassador Calvares vehicle stopped a few hundred feet behind the C-17 and Lydia recognized Tom, Dolan Domenico, Darren, and the rest of the operation team gathered by the Univision mobile unit. Tom approached the vehicle and Charlie unexpectedly opened the rear door and jumped out. He ran towards his dad screaming "daddy, daddy!"

Tom embraced him in a tight hug that lasted over a minute.

"Are you ok champ?" he asked Charlie

"Yes I am daddy, and you?" Charlie asked him

"I'm just fine young man. I love you so much. And I am so, so proud of you son" Tom said as he gave Charlie kisses all over his face.

Lydia slowly approached them letting father and son enjoy their moment. She stopped close to Tom and Charlie and then asked him "How did I do honey?"

"You did a great job babe. You are my hero Lydia" Tom said

They held each other and kissed while Charlie smiled at them.

"Did they get what they needed?" asked Lydia

"Don't know yet hun. We will have to analyze the translation. But don't worry about that now. Come on, we need to get out of here" Tom replied as they quickly stepped up the ramp of the cargo plane. Before leaving, Domenico was conveying his appreciation to the Univision mobile unit driver. He tapped the hood of the mobile unit and said to the driver

"*Gracias Julián. Hablaremos más tarde*" [Thanks Julián. Will talk to you later]. The mobile unit then quickly sped away and disappeared into the darkness.

The four powerful Pratt and Whitney engines of the C-17 started running as the rest of the team ran to the back of the transport plane and each one started to strap to their seats. Dolan Domenico approached the Winston family.

"You did a fantastic job Lydia" Dolan said loudly as the noise of the C-17 engines muffled his voice

"Thank you Dolan" Lydia screamed back

"Let's go home guys" he said to the Winstons "sorry I could not fly you all first class" he added

"Don't worry sir. Just get us back home safe" Tom yelled back

"You bet your ass I will" Dolan replied

After everyone was inside the plane the giant ramp slowly started to close and the noise of the powerful engines dwindled down.

"You all did a great job folks. Secretary Donovan would be proud of this great team. Thank you all again" Dolan said

Dolan strapped himself next to Lydia. Lydia was looking for that strange woman who had helped them at Carondelet Palace. After finding where she was seated she said to her "hey, thanks for the help out there earlier. And for protecting me and my son. Sorry I did not ask your name earlier. Too much going on out there"

"Don't worry Mrs. Winston. No need to apologize. Just doing my job. My name is Alex Harpster. CIA"

The C-17 stood still with the engines running for more than ten minutes. Lydia turned to Dolan and gave him a worried smile.

"I'll go see what the hold up is. We'll be ok" Dolan tried to re-assure Lydia. But Lydia did not reply. She only gripped Charlie's hand.

Dolan Domenico got up from his seat and entered the cockpit.

"What is the hold up gentlemen?" he asked the flight crew

A United States Air Force captain in his mid twenties replied to Dolan "They grounded all flights out of Quito airport sir. Tower says we must stay put until further instructions"

"They must be referring to commercial flights captain. We are not a commercial airline, are we?" Dolan asked the C-17 captain

"Well... no sir, we are not..." the captain agreed

"Well then... get this plane on the air captain. We must leave now, do you read me?" Dolan said affirmatively

"But sir, Quito control tower stated that it was a national security measure"

"Believe me captain, when I say to you, it is not because of a national security measure. Turn around captain. Do you see that woman sitting next to that boy?" Dolan asked pointing to Lydia and Charlie.

"Yes sir. I do see them"

"Well captain. That's who they are looking for. That's who they want. Do you want that woman and her son tortured by the fucking Russians?" Domenico asked

"Of course not sir" the captain answered back

"Do you want that kid see his mother tortured in front of him?" Dolan asked again

"No sir. Of course not!" the captain replied disturbed

"Then, for god's sake and their safety captain, get this plane on the air! I don't give a shit what Quito tower says!"

The young captain looked at his first officer seating to his right and said to him "let's do it Mike" he ordered

"Yes sir. Let's go home captain" the first officer replied

"Thank you gentlemen" Dolan said softly and then returned to his seat

The C-17 transport started to taxi to the active runway when right away a call from the Quito control tower came in.

"Heavy 352. This is Quito International tower. Are you aware of the takeoff restrictions? Over?"

"Don't answer Mike" the captain said to his first officer

After no response from the C-17 crew another call came into the cockpit from Quito control tower.

"Heavy 352. I repeat, they are take off restrictions at this time for all flights out of Quito International. Do you copy? Over?"

Mike looked at the captain and shook his head. The C-17 cargo plane continued slowly taxing to the runway when a third call came from the Quito control tower.

"Heavy 352. I say again, all outbound flights are grounded until further notice by order of the President of the Republic of Ecuador. Do you understand? Over?"

"Let me handle this cap" Mike said

"Go for it Mike"

The first officer positioned his mike close to his mouth and then clearly replied to Quito control tower "no hablo español, no comprendo, tower"

After Mike's reply a different voice this time came over their headsets from Quito control tower with a new demand.

"Heavy 352. This is Quito International control tower again. I am immediately instructing you to return your plane to your starting point. This is a direct order from the President of Ecuador. I know you can understand my English very well, Heavy 352. Do you copy, over?"

By this time the C-17 had reached the end of the runway. The captain applied full thrust to the Pratt and Whitney engines and the United States Air Force C-17 cargo plane started to roll down the runway. As the plane got airborne and the wheels went up the fuselage the captain decided to respond finally to Quito control tower.

"Quito control tower, this is Heavy 352. We do not answer to the President of Ecuador. We answer to the President of the United States. Adiós amigos. Over and out"

The captain then turned to Dolan and pointed for him to put on his headsets.

"Where to sir?" he asked him

"Panamanian airspace captain" replied Dolan Domenico

"Copy that sir" the captain answered

15

They all safely arrived the next morning at Edwards Air Force base in California. Dolan Domenico, Darren Johnson, and the Winston family were transferred right away to a flight to Virginia where the transcripts of the recordings would be analyzed and scrutinized by the CIA and FBI intelligence analysts. They were all scrambling to make sense of what was on Perchenko's mind and desperately trying to figure out his next move as the Russian fleet slowly entered Ecuadorian waters. Everyone at both agencies was working tirelessly to prevent a crisis not seen since the Kennedy Presidency, or worse, a conflict between the two nuclear superpowers. The day after arriving on U..S. soil FBI agent Tom Winston woke early that morning and visited Dolan Domenico's office searching for the latest news. He knocked softly on the door.

"Good morning agent Winston" Dolan greeted him

"Good morning sir"

"Too early to be here Tom. I'm going to have to explain your absences to your new field office trainer"

"No problem sir. I already called them. Any news sir?" he asked

"No. Not yet. They are examining the recordings and agent Johnson is also assisting" replied Dolan

"I'm available too if you need me sir"

"No agent Winston. You and your family have done enough. Let the analysts do their jobs. Hopefully they will find out something concrete soon"

Their chat was interrupted when Darren entered Domenico's office with a handful of documents in his hands.

"Good morning gentlemen" he greeted both

"Hello Darren. Nice to see you again my friend" said Tom

"Nice to see you too Tom" Darren answered shaking Tom's hand

"Do you have something for me son? Time is of the essence" Dolan interrupted

"May have something sir"

"May? As in a wild ass guess? Is that what you mean agent Johnson? Not sure?"

"Sir, let me explain. From the recordings we captured from Mrs. Winston, we are trying to figure out the wording of Perchenko's thoughts. Especifically, what did Lydia meant when she said quote, *you all will be in complete darkness,* unquote" Darren concluded reading from one of the many documents on hand. He then continued "Is Perchenko planning a nuclear strike, is he referring to a wide cyber attack blacking out all major systems in our country, or some type of chemical warfare attack? Many people on both agencies have been working around the clock trying to decipher his thoughts. I may have stumbled on to something interesting"

"Well, what is it?" Dolan asked anxious

"About ten hours ago sir, a Navy Seal Team was launched from the Virginia class submarine USS John Warner. They were able to get close enough to three of the Russian ships from the fleet entering the Ecuadorian waters undetected. After they returned to the USS John Warner they reported something unusual" said Darren

"What did they find?" asked Dolan Domenico

"Well sir, is not what they found, but rather what they did not"

"What the hell you mean?"

"Sir, according to the Seal Team they did not detect any alpha or beta particles, or any gamma rays emanating from any of the Russian vessels"

"What does that mean in English son?" Dolan asked

"Sir, it means that is very possible that none of these Russian ships are carrying any nuclear missiles" Darren replied

"What? What the fuck are you saying agent Johnson?" Dolan asked now somewhat confused

"Like I said sir, it looks like the Russian fleet may not be equipped with any nuclear weapons after all"

After his response Dolan approached Darren and extended his open left hand palm to him and told him "let me see that damn report. This does not make any sense"

"It does not make any sense to me either Darren. Why would Perchenko play it like that risking a nuclear conflict with the United States with empty guns?" Tom asked Darren

Dolan was quietly flipping thru the pages of the report marked *TOP SECRET- NEED TO KNOW ONLY*. After glancing at the report, he stood up from his chair.

"Why in the hell would Perchenko play chicken with us, knowing what the consequences could be? Why? Can you explain that to me? Any of you? Any idea?"

"This is nonsense! Is Perchenko that crazy, out of his fucking mind Darren?" asked Tom

"Well, I may have an answer to that too" replied Darren

"There is that word again...may? This is too much speculation son. We cannot afford that""said Dolan shaking his head

"Sir, I strongly believe Perchenko was playing us all along. I believe it was all a distraction..."

"Distraction? Hold on agent Johnson" Dolan said with a sarcastic laugh

"Are you telling me that President Perchenko's plans to send ships to Ecuador and the possible deployment of mobile nuclear capable ballistic missiles in the Galapagos Islands was all a show, a mere distraction? For what?" asked Dolan

"Yes sir...that is what I think" Darren responded

"But why Darren?" added Tom

"Here, I'll show you" Darren answered fumbling thru more of his top secret classified papers. "I obtained intelligence from a friend of mine at the CIA. It appears that our friend Perchenko has been playing another card since those ships started sailing to the coast of Ecuador. You see this place in this Russian map?" Darren asked both Tom and Dolan

"What about it?" Tom asked him

"Well, this place here" Darren started pointing at the Russian map "it is called the Plesetsk Cosmodrome, about eight hundred kilometers north of Moscow. It was originally an ICBM site, but lately it has been a very busy place, with the launch of an anti-satellite missile as early as 2016. My colleague at the CIA tells me that our satellites have detected lots of activity here ever since this whole crisis started with the Ecuadorian government. They suspect an imminent launch of another newer, and much more powerful anti-satellite missile soon"

"Keep going son, You have my full attention" said Dolan as he attentively listened to Darren

"Mine too" added Tom

"Gentlemen, it is my professional opinion that Perchenko's plan all along was to destroy one of our satellites with a launch from the Plesetsk site. And, I am very confident to add that the Russian fleet scenario was a mere distraction for us and the world, in order to hide his real intentions"

"Holy shit! Are you kidding me?" Tom asked perplexed

"I'm afraid not, my dear friend" replied Darren

Dolan Domenico then looked straight at Darren and asked him "Agent Johnson, can you give me a percentage of how sure you are about this?"

"I would say sir... more than ninety percent certainty sir"

"Why?" asked Dolan

"Going again back to Mrs. Winston recordings at Carondelet Palace; remember when she said quote *'your President is so preoccupied with my ships at the coast of Ecuador that your American friends and families will not know what hit them'* unquote? I am sure Perchenko was referring to the destruction of one of our satellites"

Tom then interrupted and said "but Darren, hold on. You are talking about only one of our satellites. We have hundreds in space"

"Agent Winston has a good point agent Johnson" said Dolan

"Yes Tom. It is only one satellite I am referring to. But this one is not your usual satellite"

"What do you mean Darren?" asked Tom

"You will both understand after I explain to you both the Zeus classified program. Or, as many call it, MOAS, for Mother Of All Satellites" Darren answered

"Let's hear it Darren" said Tom

"Back in 2010, our Defense Department decided to create a top secret project called Zeus, named after the mythological Greek character. Here, I was able to obtain an overview of the project" Darren continued saying handling a folder marked *TOP SECRET* in red and titled *Master Synchronization for Department of Defense Satellite Network System* to Dolan Domenico.

"Hum… go on…" Dolan said

"Zeus was placed at the highest orbit of any known satellite"

"How high is that?" Tom asked

"Usually most of our satellites orbit on what they call geosynchronous orbit, that's around twenty two thousand miles above earth. Zeus was placed over seven thousand miles above geosynchronous orbit at almost thirty thousand miles above earth. Gentlemen, Zeus is the master synchronizer for all of the Department of Defense satellites that orbit below him"

"And, you think this is what Perchenko is really after?"

"Yes sir. I really do" assured Darren

"Do you really think his new anti-satellite missile can reach that high?" Dolan inquired

"A few years ago, they did not have that capability. But now I believe they do. Plus the Russians have been getting a lot of technological help on this area from the Chinese also"

Dolan hesitated some before asking his next question, then he said "tell me, agent Johnson. What would happen if this Russian missile happens to knock down Zeus?"

Darren took a long pause before answering Dolan. He took a long, deep breath.

"All of Zeus children satellites will loose synchronization rendering them useless. All communications from all of our Defense Department satellites will be lost, sir"

"What? Are you kidding me? For how long?" asked Dolan surprised

"At least for seventy two hours. Or more, until Space Command can synchronize all satellites, one by one"

"Please tell me we have a backup for this thing..."

"I am afraid not sir. When Zeus was launched in 2010 the team that worked on this project saw no need for a backup back then. They did not worry of any anti-satellite missile being able to reach Zeus. But times and technology has quickly changed making Zeus vulnerable now. Also, our politicians did not want to spend an estimated three billion dollars more on the project. They wanted to use the money for other things" Darren explained

"Yep. Like building a wall...right?" Tom said

"Amen to that my friend" Darren replied

"Jesus almighty! Are you saying that all of our defense communications will be in the dark for at least three days?" Dolan asked

"Well... not only that sir. If Zeus is destroyed there is a strong possibility that some of our satellites might de orbit, creating somewhat of a space highway crash as Zeus children satellites bump into each other"

"This means no communication or links of any kind. Not even with Air Force One. Complete darkness" Tom suggested

"I'm afraid so Tom. And I think seventy two hours is being conservative, to tell you the truth..."

"Just as Lydia said when she was at Carondelet Palace sir. Complete darkness" Tom said glancing curiously at Dolan

"What? What are you thinking Tom?" asked Dolan

Tom stood up and started pacing back and forth in front of Dolan's desk. He suddenly stopped, took a glance at Darren then at Dolan Domenico. He pointed his index finger at Dolan and said to him "what if...sir... what if the Russian fleet was not a distraction as Darren explained, but instead, a part of the puzzle of Perchenko's diabolical plan?" he asked

"What plan is that Tom?" Darren asked

"Well, as you said Darren, we will be in complete communications darkness for at least seventy two hours. Correct?"

"Yes. That is correct" Darren answered him

"Think about it. Currently, the Russian fleet is just three thousand miles from the California coast. What if, Perchenko's plan is to invade the western United States while all of our satellites are down? What if, all of those crazy news regarding a western invasion are not so crazy after all?"

"That SOB wouldn't dare!" Dolan said angrily

"I think he would sir. Not so far fetched. After all, Hitler tried it in Europe, until he got too greedy" Darren replied

"But before he can proceed with his crazy plan, he must disable Zeus so we will be vulnerable for at least three days. We will be seating ducks" Dolan said

"That's right sir" said Darren

"How can we stop this madness? Any ideas?" Tom asked

"Don't know yet agent Winston. But let me assure you. I will be damned if I'll let that happen. I am sure you both agree with me that we do not want to see Russian tanks roaring thru the streets of Los Angeles. Over my dead body!" Dolan exclaimed

Before Tom or Darren could reply to Dolan's comment a young man came walking fast down the hallway and stopped by Dolan's door.

"Have you heard sir?" he asked poking his head halfway thru the door

"No. What is it?"

"Mallory got canned. It will be disclosed at a press briefing tomorrow morning" the young man said to Dolan

"Did they say why?" Dolan asked him

"Something about him not being suitable for the position. And, it looks like a lot of people despised him"

"Well, I sure don't feel sorry for the little shit"

"Oh... another thing sir. This report also just came in. Hot of the press" the young agent said handling Dolan a single sheet of paper

"What is this?"

"Something about lots of activity at this...site in Russia called ple... something, captured by our satellites"

"You mean Plesetsk?" Darren asked with a worried look on his face

"Yea...that. Everything ok sir?" the young agent asked after seeing the look on Dolan's face as he was reading the single page report

"Yes son. All is fine. Thanks for the info. You can go now"

Dolan stared at the single page report for over a minute and then glanced at Tom and Darren.

"Shit! It has started! Tom, Darren. Notify all of our intelligence agencies of our findings including the Carondelet Palace recordings. I need to call Simon right away" Dolan instructed

As soon as Tom and Darren had left his office Dolan dialed Simon's number on his secured phone. The now familiar voice answered and Dolan said right away "sir, I have bad news and I have bad news. Which one do you want to hear first?"

"Oh shit!..." Dolan heard Simon said at the other end of the line.

16

Before becoming the new elected President of Russia Nikolai Perchenko had already made billions investing in the rich oil fields of his country. He was listed on the Forbes magazine with an estimated net worth of over fifteen billion dollars, but his real net worth was a mystery for many. He kept a low profile when it came to his business ventures and he was known to be a great father and husband who loved to spoil his family often. They were many stories of him purchasing expensive jewelry for his wife Alana, at one time spending ten million dollars on a one of a kind diamond and rubies necklace. He loved to spoil his son and daughter as well, Marco and Alexandra, ages thirteen and sixteen, sending them at times on exotic safaris and world tours sometimes lasting for months at a time. That is why when his wife Alana wanted to purchase a vacation property in New York city only the best location would suffice. She wanted luxury, privacy, and security for her and her family when traveling to the big apple. After looking for over two months they settle on a penthouse at the Woolworth Tower Residences, one of the most luxurious and prestigious addresses in New York city. The price was ninety eight million dollars for the almost ten thousand square feet spread at the top of the iconic building. A simple wire transfer from one of her husband's many companies took care of the purchase. Perchenko was at the top of the world, with billions on his bank accounts, a beautiful loving family, and now as President of his country. For Perchenko, it would be an astute and excellent investment of what it would become part of the greater Russian empire. But for many powerful men, power can be so intoxicating that it can lead to blindness. And for Nikolai Perchenko, one of the most powerful figures on the world, one thing would derail his plans for conquest. His ego.

Back in his office Dolan was answering a call back from Simon after he had shared the latest intel provided by FBI agent Darren Johnson.

"That son of a bitch has gone wacko" said Simon

"I agree sir. How do we stop him?" asked Dolan

"Well Dolan, as they say, desperate times call for desperate measures"

"And that means?..."

""That means that our President will not stand still while Perchenko tries to cripple our satellite defense systems and tries to invade our country. If he wants to play dirty, we will gladly comply and play dirty too" explained Simon

"Does that mean a preemptive nuclear strike?" Dolan asked

"No, we don't want nuclear armageddon. At least not yet. We will pursue other options to persuade him to change his mind"

"So, what's the plan sir?"

"The President has authorized a special team to go after what Perchenko holds most dear" Simon answered Dolan

"His money?" Dolan asked

"No, Dolan. His family"

"His family? Where, at the Kremlin?"

"No. We know that they recently purchased a very expensive penthouse in Manhattan from a billionaire friend of them. His wife and children have been vacationing there for some time now, and spending lavishly" Simon noted

Dolan breathed deep, and then scratched his left temple before he asked Simon "are you saying sir...to take them hostages?"

It took a little while for Simon to answer Dolan back. He finally said to him "not only that Dolan"

"Say again sir?" Dolan asked perplexed

There was another pause from Simon before he continued.

"We are authorized to execute all of them. While he watches, one by one, if that is what it would take for him to change his crazy plans"

"This...authorized by our Commander in Chief?"

"Authorized, but of course not traced back to the President Dolan. Like a told you earlier, desperate times..."

"Calls for desperate measures..." Dolan interrupted Simon

"Whatever it takes to prevent this madman from launching that anti-satellite missile. Whatever it takes Dolan"

"I'll have to say sir, that is way, way out there"

"It's either his family, or our country Dolan"

"I... I... agree sir"

"Goodbye Dolan"

"Goodbye Simon"

After ending his call with Simon Dolan slowly put his phone down. It was hard even for him, a man that had seen so much tragedy and suffering during his service in Vietnam to comprehend how egotistical and evil one single person could be. Enough to completely change the political landscape of a country and the future of all of its citizens. He stared at one of the pictures on his desk. It was of a group of seven of his friends when stationed in Hanoi. Some of them were still alive, others had perished. Seating on his office chair he rested his elbows on his desk, and then clasped both of his hands in front of him. He had never done this, but he realized that now was the right time to do it. He leaned his head forward, and rested his forehead on his clasped hands. Then, he closed his eyes and started praying.

17

The Perchenko's had purchased the penthouse at the historic and iconic Woolworth tower, conceived by Frank Woolworth, the founder of the thrifty stores that carried his last name. It was completed in 1913 and sits on the exclusive Tribeca neighborhood of New York city. The asking price was originally one hundred ten million dollars for the nine thousand seven hundred plus square feet property that was referred to as The Pinnacle by the real estate marketing firm that was selling the penthouse. The offer from the Perchenko family was ninety eight million dollars in cash and it was accepted two days later. Alana Perchenko was ecstatic to have a place in the United States where she and her children could visit, relax, and shop at the exclusive Manhattan shops. It was a beautiful and cool evening in New York city and Alana had planned a day to go shopping and have an exquisite dinner with Marco and Alexandra. She picked up her purse and was about to call for her driver when the doorbell rang. She looked at the security camera monitor and saw her personal bodyguard's face. He pressed a button on the intercom and asked him "yes? what is it George?"

"Mrs. Perchenko, there has been a gas leak at one of the apartments below us... they... want to evacuate all tenants for safety" George answered

"Oh my god! Right now?"

"Yes ma'am. I'm afraid so" he replied

"Hold on, let me get my children" Alana said

Less than a minute later Alana was at the front door with Marco and Alexandra. She entered the security code on the keypad and the lock disengaged unlocking the front door. As soon as the door opened George was shoved in into the penthouse followed by four men all dressed in black, with black gloves and masks covering their faces except their eyes. Each of the men was carrying a nine millimeter handgun on their hands, with a belt around their waists, holding two extra fifteen bullet magazines and a six inch hunting knife. One of the men immediately hog tied George and covered his mouth with a wide piece of duct tape. Another one put his index finger in front of his mouth to indicate to Alana not to make a sound. He then grabbed Alana while the other two grabbed a hold of Alexandra and Marco. Each of the intruders brought a chair from the dinner table and forced each one to seat facing them.

The men did not say anything for a few seconds and just stared at Alana, Marco, and Alexandra. The one facing Alana then said to her "give me your mobile phone Mrs. Perchenko" he said speaking in Russian. Alana started reaching into her purse for her phone when the man pointed the nine millimeter gun at her face.

"Slowly, very slowly. And hand it to me" he told her

Alana pulled out her iPhone from her purse shaking uncontrollably and now crying

"Please, please don't hurt us, please! You can have the phone. Here, it's the latest iPhone, worth at least one thousand two hundred dollars. You can have it, here! I have some cash too, and my credit cards. You can have it all!" she cried

The man in front of Marco signaled to him to surrender his phone also. Marco slowly and carefully reached into his back pocket with his right hand and did as he demanded. The third man then asked Alexandra for hers. She was a feisty, spoiled, and rebellious sixteen year old. Unlike her brother who was crying and shaking along with his mom she challenged her assailant.

"Go get it yourself you fuckhead! My dad is going to cut you and your whole family into little pieces!" she screamed at him

After Alexandra's refusal the man in front of her slapped her hard with his backhand on the right side of her face and then hard again with his open palm on her left. A trickle of blood came out of Alexandra's mouth and a small cut appeared on her right cheek. The man was about to punch her on her face face again when Alana let out a scream.

"No, no! Please! Alexandra, please give him your stupid phone. Please, please, don't hurt her, please!" Alana implored

"You animals! Ouch! That hurts!" Alexandra started saying "it's... it's on the small gold table by the window. There!" she said pointing.

"What do you all want?" Alexandra cried

"Don't worry honey" Alana said to her daughter crying "all they want is money. They will get what they came for and then they will leave us alone. Right?" she finished saying looking at the man in front of her.

The fourth man who had hog tied their security guard came close to them with the roll of duct tape. Each of the men then reached into a black bag and took out three heavy duty plastic tie downs and proceeded to tie their victims to the chairs. Then they covered Marco and Alexandra's mouth with duct tape. All three were crying and shaking out of control as they realized that this was not just a robbery intrusion. They were afraid for their lives. After they were tied to the chairs two of the men stood right behind Alexandra and Marco. The man who was standing behind Alana kneeled behind her and whispered on her right ear "now, listen to me very carefully Mrs. Perchenko. I am going to free your hands. Do you understand me?" he said to her. Alana shook her head up and down.

"Please, please, don't hurt my children. I beg you!" she cried

"That depends on you Mrs. Perchenko"

"I'll do whatever you want, but please don't hurt them!" Alana cried again

"Here. here is your phone. This is what I want you to do Mrs. Perchenko. I want you to call your husband using your facetime app. Do you understand?"

"My husband? You want me to call my husband?" Alana replied unsure of the intruder's demands

"Yes. That's what I said. Call your husband using your video app on your phone. No tricks. No call to 911. If you don't do as I say we will start cutting your son's toes, one by one. Are we clear?"

"Yes, yes! We are clear. I will facetime my husband right now" Alana said

As soon as the call started the man behind Alana tied her hands back behind the chair, covered her mouth with duct tape, and took away her iPhone. Nikolai Perchenko's image came into view on Alana's iPhone.

"Hello honey. How are you and the children doing? Are you all enjoying New York..." he started saying. He stopped talking when he saw the images of Alana, Marco, and Alexandra's faces. The phone was moving in front of each of them showing a closeup of their horrified faces with each assailant holding a six inch hunting knife under their throats.

"What the hell? What is going on? What the fuck is this? Who is inside the penthouse? What have you done to my daughter? I swear, if you hurt any in my family I will feed you to my dogs, whoever the fuck you are! You fucking scumbag! You and your friends and families will spend the rest of your lives in a gulag in Siberia! I swear on my mother's grave!" Perchenko screamed furiously after seeing the phone video. As he was about to start another outburst the call got cut off and the video disappeared. A few seconds later the facetime call rang again in Perchenko's personal phone. It was Alana's face again, her face full of tears, breathing erratically with duct tape still on her mouth, a hand holding the six inch knife below her throat. This time a male voice said "are you done with your outbursts mister President? Want me to hang up and call you later?" he asked Nikolai Perchenko speaking in fluent Russian.

"No, no! Don't hang up!" Perchenko yelled back

"Good. Now let's talk like adults"

"What the fuck you want? Money...I have plenty of money. I will give you whatever you want and then you can let my family go. How much do you want?" asked Perchenko

"I do not want your fucking money mister President" the man replied

""You low life piece of shit! What the hell do you want then? Why do you want to hurt my family?"

"We will not hurt your family President Perchenko, if you comply with our demands"

"Demands? what demands?"

"President Perchenko, listen to me very carefully if you want to see your family alive ever again. We want you to order a total withdrawal of all of your Russian ships currently on Ecuadorian waters and return to their headquarters in Russia. Second, we demand the immediate suspension of all activity at the Plesetsk site and cancellation of any future launches of your country anti-satellite missiles. And third, Russia must give access to a group of international inspectors selected by the United Nations to confirm the dismantling of the Plesetsk Cosmodrome in order to prevent any future anti-satellite missile launches. Did you get all that President Perchenko?" the man ended explaining

"And...if I don't?" Perchenko asked the man in black

"Then, your family will experience a horrible and slow painful death. We will start with your son by cutting his extremities, one by one, then we will do the same to your daughter, and finally to your beautiful wife. We will record it all for you to see what your ego did to your family"

"How did you know about the Plesetsk Cosmodrome? Did your American President put you up to this?" Perchenko asked angrily

"That does not matter President Perchenko. What does matter is that is up to you if you want to see you family alive again"

"But...your demands...about the inspectors from the United Nations. That may take months to complete"

"Don't you worry mister President. Your family will be well taken care off. They will be our guests at an undisclosed location. As soon as we have assurance that the Plesetsk site is no longer a threat to us and other countries we will release your family. And please mister President, let me warn you, that any attempt to find out their location or try any type of rescue and we will return them to you in little pieces. Do you understand?"

"How can I trust you with the lives of my family?"

"Please mister President, don't you lecture me about trust. After all you have done, the ones concerned about trust should be us. I will give you my word your family will be returned to you alive if, and only if you comply with our demands"

By now Perchenko's attitude and demeanor had drastically changed. He was not the same man that was thirsty for power and conquering ambitions. Now, he realized that he held the lives of all of his family on his hands. Money, power, ambitions, status. None of it he cared for now. He only wanted to have back the one thing most dear to him. His family.

He sunk on his chair staring at his phone while the man in black at the other end of the line inside The Pinnacle ninety eight million dollar penthouse moved Alana's phone side to side so Perchenko could take a good look at his loving family tied and gagged.

"It is up to you President Perchenko. The time is ticking"

"How much time do I have?" asked Perchenko

"We want the first two demands within twenty four hours. Or we will start with your son"

"Wait...wait...please. What is your name? What do I call you?" asked Perchenko calmly now

"You can call us the Second Revolution Organization or SRO" We will be in touch mister President" the SRO leader answered as he ended the call and the phone screen went blank.

Perchenko tried desperately to call back Alana's phone or his childrens but to no avail. All of their lines had been compromised by the SRO members. Perchenko slammed his phone hard on his desk and let out a scream so hard that it reverberated all across his Kremlin's office. It was so loud that his personal secretary entered his office without permission thinking that the President was having a heart attack. As she entered his office she found President Perchenko standing up with his arms locked, palms on his desk and his head down.

"Are you alright mister President?" she asked him

Perchenko did not answer her. He stayed at this position for a few more seconds. All of a sudden, he stood up straight, with his arms straight to his sides and his fists clenched. He then turned to his secretary and yelled "give me Admiral Abramov on the phone, now!"

"Yes mister President. Right away!" his secretary quickly replied

18

Lydia was preparing lunch for Charlie before taking him to his school when she was distracted by the breaking news from the local CBS Network. Apparently there had been a big new development concerning the Russian and Ecuadorian crisis. After Lydia heard the news she screamed at Tom from the first floor.

"Tom, did you hear?"

"What honey?" What is it?" Tom asked coming down the stairs.

"The ships, the Russian Navy is pulling out all ships from Ecuadorian waters" said Lydia excited

"Is that so?" Tom replied

"It looks like the crisis has been averted after all honey. That is great!" she exclaimed back

"It sure is babe. That is very good news"

"Is it related to what we did at Carondelet Palace you think?"

"I'm sure it did Lydia. The recordings must have revealed something" Tom said

"Are you proud of me?" asked Lydia fixing Tom's tie

Tom was about to give her a kiss when unexpectedly Lydia turned her head away towards the television

"Shhh…" Lydia said turning her attention to the news once again. "Looks like the Secretary of State is giving a news conference dear"

"Gee...! When did you get so interested on international politics babe?" Tom asked

"Since me and Charlie became heroes" Lydia replied

Tom let out a soft smile and poured himself a cup of coffee.

"Here he comes Tom. Sit, sit..." she ordered Tom

Secretary of State Finley walked to the podium and started his speech to the press.

"Ladies and gentlemen of the press, as of zero four hundred eastern time the Russian Federation has started the withdrawal of all of its Northern Fleet ships that were anchored on the coast of Ecuador. President Perchenko has assured the United States government that their Navy military exercises have come to a conclusion and that their mission has been accomplished. The Russian government has also indicated that all ships will be out of Latin American waters by the end of this week. This brings a sigh of relief and an end to tensions between our two countries that has been ongoing for weeks. We commend President Perchenko for this decision and we look forward for future productive and friendly relations between our countries. Also, today at six PM eastern time the President of the United States will be having a press conference and answer any questions from the press. Thank you all very much for your time" the Secretary concluded saying

"I wonder what really made Perchenko changed his mind honey? What do you think?" asked Lydia

"Don't really know Lydia. But believe me, our government can be very persuasive sometimes. Maybe they gave him an offer he couldn't refuse" Tom answered

"Maybe...I guess. Well, I'm so happy this crisis is over and that we all can sleep a little better dear"

"Hey... I almost forgot to tell you. My boss gave me this yesterday" Tom said showing Lydia a plain, legal size envelope.

"What is it Tom?" asked Lydia

"Well, mister Domenico said that we all deserve a well earned vacation. Then he just handed me this envelope" said Tom laying the white envelope on the breakfast nook table. "But he said not to open it until two days before our flight"

"And when is that?"

"Ten days from now" Tom answered

"What? How are we going to plan for it then?"

"He told me that all expenses are paid for. Then he specifically told me for us to pack enough clothes for two weeks. He said that keeping it a surprise until almost the last day would make it more exciting. By the way, he is meeting us there too...wherever we are going. He is leaving two days before we do" Tom explained

"He is going too?"

"Yes honey. I think Dolan finally realized he deserves a vacation too, especially after all that has happened lately" said Tom

"Wow! That was so sweet of him. I'm sorry I called him some bad names. He is a good man after all"

"Yes he is Lydia. Well, I better go honey. Don't want to be late to my new field office" Tom said as he put on his jacket

"Have a great day at work honey"

Tom gave Lydia a kiss and then said "you too babe. Love you lots"

"I love you too honey"

Before leaving Tom screamed towards the top of the stairs

"See you later champ, dad is leaving to work" he yelled at Charlie

"See you later dad. Love you" Charlie yelled back from his upstairs room

After Tom left Lydia came back into the kitchen and stared at that white envelope laying on top of the breakfast nook table, and felt an itch to open it and find out where they were meeting Dolan Domenico. Lydia thought of exotic places such as Paris, India, Australia, maybe Japan, or the exotic Borneo. Although she felt almost compelled to open it she did not want to spoil it for Tom and Charlie. She decided after all, that not knowing was the most exciting part of the trip. She carefully picked up the envelope, flipped it four times, then placed it back on the table. By this time Charlie had come down from his room ready for his breakfast.

"I am hungry mom" Charlie said to Lydia

"Ok honey. What do you want to eat?"

"Can I have pancakes mom?" Charlie asked her

"Sure you can Charlie"

Lydia started to gather the pancake ingredients with her back towards Charlie. All of a sudden, Charlie surprised her when he grabbed her around her waist in a firm hug. He then said to her

"I love you mom. You are my hero" Charlie said

Lydia turned around and with tears on her eyes she said back to Charlie "you know what Charlie? You are my biggest hero too! I love you son" she said giving him a strong hug and a kiss on his forehead. Lydia then said to Charlie,

"You know what Charlie? What about if we just eat the pancakes, and you can skip school for today"

"Really mom? Where are we going?" asked Charlie with excitement

"I think, me and you, should go shopping for new luggage" Lydia replied to Charlie as she dried her tears

19

Panamanian Azuero Peninsula
Coastal town of Pedasí, 200 miles south of Panama City

Many people say that a man is always searching for his own paradise. For Dolan Domenico he founded it in the coastal town of Pedasí, about two hundred miles south of Panama City, Panama. It's beautiful beaches, charming houses, great fishing and snorkeling, and even whale watching had been attracting thousands of visitors to what many tourists and locals called the hidden gem of Panama. Dolan was seating in the front porch of the house by the beach calmly sipping a cold beer. There, he waited for the arrival of the Winston family to enjoy their well deserved two week vacation. After relaxing in front of the porch for about twenty minutes he saw a vehicle at a distance slowly approaching. After getting closer Dolan could now distinguish the faces of Tom, Lydia and Charlie inside the car. The two thousand square feet home was in a neighborhood called *Los Destiladeros,* very popular among American retired expats. The house roof was built with bright red Spanish tile, and a huge double wood door greeted all who entered. Situated just a few steps from the beach it was the perfect place for Dolan Domenico to relax, unwind, and enjoy his long awaited vacation.

"Glad you all could make it agent Winston" Dolan yelled to Tom from the porch, still sitting with beer in hand

"Hello sir. I see you are enjoying your time already" Tom yelled back at him

Dolan answered back by simply raising up his cold beer. Dolan then got up from his chair and proceeded to greet them.

"How are you all doing?" Had a good flight?"

"It was great Dolan. Much better than I expected" Lydia said

Dolan gave a hug to both Tom and Lydia and then turned to greet Charlie.

"And you young man? How are you doing?"

"Fine" Charlie simply answered back

"Well, get your luggage and come on in"

"This is beautiful Dolan!" Lydia exclaimed after admiring the detailed wood work on the kitchen, ceiling beams, and window frames.

"Oh my god! Look at this view honey! Gorgeous!" Tom said back to Lydia after seeing the beach view.

"Make yourselves at home. This is your secret vacation. Hope you all enjoy it" said Dolan

"I'm sure we will Dolan, thanks!" Lydia said putting her bags on the floor

"You sure surprised us boss. This is an amazing place" said Tom

"It's the least I could do Tom"

"Is Darren coming too?"

"No. Darren has become somewhat of a workaholic. He says he wants to become FBI Director within the next fifteen years"

"Hmm...that's Darren..." Tom replied

"Heard anything about President Melancón since the crisis ended?" asked Tom

"The intel we received says he may have fled to Venezuela. Others say his opposition may have gotten to him first. Either way, the people from Ecuador deserve better than him"

"I agree sir, for sure" Tom agreed, then he added,

"Tell me sir, how did you find about this place?"

"Well, after the threat to the Panama Canal during the crisis I started reading more about the country itself. Then, I called a few local realtors, talked to some Americans living here, they gave me a few suggestions of where to visit, and here we are" Dolan explained

"Can we...look around?" Lydia asked Dolan

"Sure Lydia, go ahead. *Mi casa es su casa*" replied Dolan with a soft smile

Lydia grabbed Charlie and they started exploring the beach home while Tom was still enjoying the unobstructed view of the beach from the living room.

"This...is a vacation home. You sure hit a home run with this one"

"Yes. I hope so. Very quiet and small community away from the big city"

"I see you have quite a few things here" Tom said looking around "looks like you are settling very well boss. How long are you planning to stay here?" asked Tom

"Don't know"

"What? Don't know?"

"It depends on what the sea tells me Tom"

"The sea tells you?" asked Tom confused

"I officially retired son. This is my place now" Dolan answered

"What? You mean, you bought this property?"

"Yes Tom. This is my new home now. No more big city noise, traffic, smog, or crime to worry about"

"Good for you sir. It was well due" said Tom

"Thanks Tom"

Tom started to look at some pictures Dolan had placed on a wood shelf on a wall. One specific picture caught his attention. It was one of Dolan with a group of soldiers when stationed in Vietnam. He took a closer look.

"Sir, this picture. I am curious. This man, right here behind you. He looks familiar." inquired Tom

"Oh...yes. A group of my men before heading out for another recon mission in that hell hole" Dolan replied

"But the man behind you, this one" Tom inquired again pointing at the specific man on the picture "he sure looks like Defense Secretary Donovan"

"You are very attentive to detail son"

"Well, is that him sir?" Tom asked

"Yes he is. He was our commander while I was stationed at the hell hole. He was a two star general back then before he decided to get into politics. We became very close friends, looked after each other"

"You mean, you are still, close friends…"

"You can say that…"

"Close enough of a friend for you to obtain inside intel"

Dolan did not answer Tom and instead took a gulp of his beer. Tom then asked him "he is the secretive Simon, isn't he?"

"Again son, you are very attentive…" Dolan started saying

"I'll be damned…!" exclaimed Tom

"But let's not worry about work right now Tom. We are here to enjoy our vacation. What do you say if we go outside and enjoy this gorgeous beach?" asked Dolan

"Sounds good to me sir" Tom replied looking back at the picture and shaking his head

Before Tom and Dolan stepped into the beach Lydia and Charlie joined them back from the tour of the home

"It's a beautiful home Dolan" Lydia said

"Well, you all are welcome to come whenever you want. I'll be waiting, right here. Going nowhere"

"Dolan bought this house honey. He decided to retire here in Panama" Tom said to Lydia

"Oh my god. That's great. I'm so happy for you Dolan"

"Thanks Lydia. But before you go play on the sand I have a couple things for you"

"What? You have done enough with this great vacation sir" said Tom

"No. It's something I owe to Charlie. Something we promised him while we were inside building 911 in Nevada"

"Owed to Charlie? Like what?" asked Lydia surprised

"Here" Dolan said handling Lydia another plain white envelope

"Is this a routine for you? Giving people white envelopes?" asked Lydia

"Only for very special persons. Inside you will find your next vacation. A one week paid trip to Disney World"

Upon hearing this Charlie jumped in excitement and asked Lydia "we are going to Disney World mom? For real?"

"Looks like honey. Thanks to mister Domenico. What do you say to him Charlie?"

"Thanks mister Domenico!" Charlie said

"No, thanks to you young man. It's the least I can do after what you have done for our country" Dolan responded

"And, what is this Dolan?" Lydia asked still looking inside the envelope

"That...is... a gift, from one of the President's biggest donors"

"Oh my god! Are you serious? Is this for real? Tom, look at this!" Lydia cried out showing Tom inside the envelope

"What the hell? A check for three million dollars sir? Is this a joke?" asked Tom

"No it's not son. After finding out what your family had done to prevent a world crisis this billionaire decided to donate this money for Charlie's future. It will be set up in a trust until Charlie reaches the age of eighteen. After that, your family can use it for his care, any needs, or education, if Charlie decides to go to college"

"We... don't know what to say sir. This is... incredible!" Tom said

"Don't worry guys. This donor has billions. It will be just a tax write off for him" said Dolan

"Can you give us his name?" asked Lydia

"No I can't. He prefers to remain anonymous. But I will sure pass along your appreciation"

"Please, please do" said Lydia handling the envelope to Tom for safekeeping. Before Lydia and Charlie were about to step on the beach Dolan's secure mobile phone rang

"Hello Simon. Is she on the secure line?" he asked

"Yes she is. Hold on... Madame President? We are on a secure line now. You may proceed ma'am" Simon said

"Hold on, Lydia, Charlie. Someone wants to talk to you" Dolan yelled

Dolan pressed the speaker icon on the secure phone and a female voice was heard

"The Winston family?" United States President Michelle Harper said on the secure line

"Yes ma'am. This is Tom Winston. An honor to be speaking with you"

"Likewise agent Winston. Is your family there agent Winston?"

"Yes they are Madame President"

"Hello President Harper. This is Lydia Winston with my son Charlie"

"I just wanted to call you and express our deepest gratitude on behalf of my administration as well as the American people for what you and Charlie have done to avert a crisis of such magnitude. We will always be indebted to your family. If there is anything that we can do in the future for any of you please let agent Domenico know. He will contact us thru the proper channels" Madame President Harper said

"Thank you Madame President" Lydia replied

"Thanks again President Harper" Tom added

"Is my young hero there?" asked the President

"Yes he is ma'am" answered Lydia

"Charlie?" President Harper asked

Lydia whispered on Charlie's ear and said "say, yes Madame President?"

"Yes, Madame President?" Charlie repeated

"Hope you can visit me after your vacation Charlie. I am looking forward to meet you young man" Lydia whispered again to Charlie "say, yes ma'am"

"Yes ma'am" Charlie repeated again

"Good. Great job from all of you. And again our deepest gratitude on behalf of our country" President Harper concluded

"Yes ma'am" Dolan, Tom, and Lydia said at the same time

After they had finished speaking with President Harper Charlie was anxious to feel the sand under his feet

"Can we go play now mom?" Charlie asked Lydia

"Yes honey. We can go now. Will see you guys in a bit. Let's go Charlie"

Charlie and Lydia hit the beach running. A few minutes later they stopped, and they started to build a sand castle.

"You have a great family Tom. And a brave woman" Dolan said to him

"I know sir"

Dolan's personal mobile phone rang and he answered

"Let yourself in, we are in the back of the house" he said

Tom looked at Dolan with a surprised look on his face wondering who else Dolan would have invited to his new beach home. Two minutes later doctor Abigail Lobowski appeared on the back porch, accompanied by a woman and a young girl.

"Glad you could come doctor" Dolan said

"Hello doctor Lobowski. How are you?" Tom asked surprised to see her.

"I am doing...great mister Winston. And...how is your family?"

"We couldn't be any better. Here, enjoying the great hospitality of mister Dolan Domenico"

"I see...I am glad to know your family...is doing well"

"Thanks doc" Tom replied

"Gentlemen, let me introduce you to Mariela Corrales and her daughter Eva"

"Hello Mariela, Eva" said Tom shaking their hands

"Nice to meet you both, ladies. A pleasure" said Dolan

"Mister Winston, Mariela and Eva... are from the country of Nicaragua... but they have been living in the United States... for the past ten years" explained doctor Lobowski

"Are they vacationing here too?" asked Tom

"Well, they are here, mister Winston, but not actually on vacation" the doctor replied

"Is that so?"

"Mariela and her daughter... Eva.. have experienced the same traits that... connect Lydia and Charlie mister Winston"

"What? Are you telling me that they...?"

"Yes, mister Winston. After extensive research...and quite a bit of travel...I have found another mother and child...with the same capabilities as Lydia and Charlie"

"Did you know about this sir?" Tom asked Dolan

"Yes, and no. The doctor contacted me about her findings but I did not meet them until now. Just like you did" Dolan said

"Mister Domenico...told me of your get together...here in Panama. So, I thought... it would be the perfect place... for them to meet you all" the doctor said

"Well sir, you sure are full of surprises lately"

"So they tell me agent Winston" Dolan replied

"Where is Lydia and Charlie... may I ask?" Lobowski asked

"Down there doc" Tom said pointing at them "building their great sand castle"

"Oh, yes. I see them. Excuse me gentlemen. I want to introduce Mariela and Eva...to Charlie and Lydia...if mister Winston does not mind..." inquired doctor Lobowski

"No, of course not doc. Go ahead, by all means" Tom said

Doctor Lobowski turned to Mariela and Eva and said to them

"Mariela, Eva, I want you to meet... two very special persons, just like you two. Come on" the doctor instructed

From the distance Tom could hear Lydia's thrilled voice upon seeing doctor Lobowski approaching her and Charlie.

"Nice to see you again doctor Lobowski. How have you been?"

"Nice to see you both. Lydia, I want you... and Charlie to meet... Mariela and her daughter Eva" Tom heard the doctor say

Tom and Dolan stayed back while doctor Lobowski introduced the new visitors to Lydia and Charlie. They could hear the laughs of Charlie and Eva as they played in the sand. After Tom watched them play for a while Tom turned to Dolan and asked him "so, sir. No plans to return to Virginia any time soon?"

"Why should I Tom? Look around you. Beautiful weather and beaches, great food, gorgeous sunsets, great fishing, and pretty good beer, may I say. What else a man needs?" responded Dolan

Dolan then abruptly extended his arms to his sides, closed his eyes, and tilt his head back. He then took a long, deep breath and said to Tom

"Do you smell that Tom? Do you smell it?" Dolan asked Tom

Tom breathed in deep and asked puzzled "no sir, I don't smell anything. What is it?"

"The smell of paradise son. The sweet smell of paradise!" Dolan replied back

THE END

Made in the USA
Middletown, DE
13 March 2023